THE ECONOMY OF LIGHT

"We must get to Manaus," he said, "and then we'll go up Rio Branco, almost to Venezuela, I think. Dangerous."

"Why?" I asked.

He looked even more uncomfortable. "It's different up there from other jungle places," he said after a time. "More dreams."

"What?"

"Dreams, they are real, like us. You can see them. They are dangerous. They can look like animals, but they aren't. You will see them if you go. You think not, but you will. Your dreams, too, will be real...."

* * * * * * *

This is the story of a Nazi hunter's journey to find the man who tortured him and murdered his family. Michael Swanwick called this extraordinary novel a "dark quest into the heart of dreams." It is a magnificent depiction of a modern descent into hell...and the frightening—and profoundly surprising—consequences of redemption.

Borgo Press Books by JACK DANN

Da Vinci Rising
The Diamond Pit: A Science Fiction Novel
The Economy of Light
Jubilee

THE ECONOMY OF LIGHT

JACK DANN

THE BORGO PRESS
MMXII

THE ECONOMY OF LIGHT

DEDICATION

For Lucius Shepard

CONTENTS

We wander in darkness now, but one with another we all have the conviction that we are advancing to the light.

—Albert Schweitzer

The physiognomy, or vertical structure, of the rain forest, is best understood in terms of the universal quest for light.

—Alex Shoumatoff

"Look there! See how the sun's shafts do not drive through to the left of that one lower down, and how he walks as if he were alive!"

—Dante's *Purgatorio*

CHAPTER ONE
LET THERE BE LIGHT

I stood by the side of the grave, along with the other reporters, photographers, doctors, police officials, and bystanders, and watched three gravediggers working with pick and shovel to exhume Josef Mengele's remains. We were in the Embu Cemetery, about twenty-five miles outside of São Paulo. The workers, dark *cafuzos* of black and Indian blood, had been digging for almost an hour. The sweat ran from their arms and faces, and the heat seemed to radiate from them in clouds. I was reminded of cars overheating in the humid mid-afternoon air.

I had arrived late, having taken the wrong exit on the eight-lane highway that leads out of São Paulo, and I felt nauseated. My stomach ached, a dull pain that had started when I had finally gotten out of my rented Saab. Before I left my hotel in São Paulo to drive here, I had wolfed down a poorly prepared *feijoada*; the beef and sausages had seemed a bit too sour. I could only hope that it wasn't too badly tainted. But it was more than the food or the weather. I was uncomfortable here because of the cold-sweat memories of childhood that intruded on this circus-like gathering.

As I looked down into the grave at the white-shirted *cafuzos* mugging for the television cameras as they chopped and dug and burrowed about four feet into the damp-smelling earth, I could almost smell the sickeningly sweet stink of Auschwitz; and I remembered being pushed out of the train and separated from my mother and brother by soldiers with snarling, snapping guard dogs. I was screaming for my mother and David, my brother, but they had both been swallowed into the frightened crowd that the soldiers were dividing into two groups. I was too short to see over the milling adults. I tried to move, but screaming people were pushing against me from all directions, as if everyone needed to stay as close together as possible, as if that was the only way to survive.

I remember looking up toward the sky and seeing a huge red brick chimney that narrowed toward the top. Thick black smoke billowed out of it, and flames rose between its lightning rods, as if conjured up from sorcerer's wands. Although I didn't recognize the smell that permeated the air, it was burning flesh and hair. I put my hands over my mouth and pinched my nose to block out the smells of death and fear and looked down intently at the dry, parched ground, which was like the surface of the moon. I repeated the *Shema Yisroel*, over and over and over. I thought that if I could narrow my focus of attention and pray with my entire being, I might be able to make the terrible noise and smell of that place disappear.... I might be able to make the camp disappear.

I was only ten years old, but I had been in a slaughterhouse before. I knew what this place was.

And that's when I saw Mengele.

I saw his boots first. They were black and polished, although covered with dust. He held my chin and raised my face upward, and he looked as large as the chimney I had seen an instant ago. He was handsome in his well-tailored SS uniform; he had an angular face, shaved clean. I noticed that there was a gap between his front teeth and he had a mole on his left cheek. He wore white gloves and, unlike everyone else, he didn't seem to be sweating. His breath smelled of cigarettes as he said, "*Zwillinge, Zwillinge?*" Was I a twin? he had asked, but I was so frightened that I could only look at him and blink. I seemed to see with a sort of tunnel vision. I noticed that there was a dull spot and a long scratch on the polished cane he held in his left hand.

"Yes," someone else said, "he's a twin. His mother and brother are in the other line."

That had saved my life. They took my brother and me to a hospital for experimentation and gassed my mother. May she rest in peace.

Then there was a shout, for the gravediggers had located the coffin, and I was jolted back to the present. I found myself whispering the *Shema*, as if from old habit, although I am not a religious Jew. The *cafuzos* dug the dirt away from the plain pine coffin, but couldn't get the top open. The police chief of São Paulo, a heavy-set man with a greased mustache, ordered them to break it open. I'd had a nodding acquaintance with this man when I worked for Mossad, the Israeli secret service. He had built up his political base of fear and power through the Brazilian intelligence bureau and was responsible for capturing Gustav Wagner, the deputy commandant of the Sobibor camp who had gassed two hundred and fifty thousand people with carbon monoxide fumes from a captured Russian tank.

One of the gravediggers smashed through the lid with his pick, and they pried it off. Inside the coffin I could see rotting shreds of clothes and a skeleton with its arms placed at its sides instead of over the chest, which was the customary manner of Brazilian burial. But The SS always buried their dead with arms at the sides, as if one should spend eternity at attention.

Several men climbed down into the grave. One of them, the São Paulo assistant coroner, a man of about sixty with short-cropped white hair, lifted up the skull and held it high for the reporters, who were feverishly snapping pictures. He turned around slowly, holding it in his outstretched hand, and when he held it toward me, I felt a wave of nausea wash over me, and the pain in my stomach became excruciating. The eye sockets and nose cavity seemed dark as tar, even in the blazing sunlight. Everything seemed to waver around me as I looked into that vertiginous darkness, and I saw the barracks when I'd lived in Camp B2f in Auschwitz. They called it the Zoo, and we called Mengele 'Uncle Pepi.' He would bring us chocolate and clothes one day and experiment on us the next. As I looked into those eye sockets, I remembered the experiments on my brother and myself—the transfusions of blood, mine to his, and vice versa; the injections every day that made us sick and feverish; and the electrical experiments, which put David into a coma. He had taken David away to the laboratory where he injected chloroform into his heart to kill him. I was to be next...for comparison. But the allies disrupted his plans by liberating us.

I could feel myself falling backward, as if the darkness was time itself and Mengele was still God, taking and giving life. His breath was the crematorium, his touch was the needle and the knife, and his voice was the last lullaby we heard. He used to sing while he worked on us. He loved Verdi and Strauss, the sonovabitch.

He had taken my family.

And I cursed him every moment for choosing my brother first.

* * * * * * *

When I regained consciousness, I found an old acquaintance, Filip Hausner, bending over me. We had worked together years ago in Paraguay and had almost caught Mengele in 1962 right here in São Paulo, but Ben-Gurion had been pressured to call off the operation because of a religious kidnapping that had threatened Israel with a civil war. Hausner and I were called back to Israel. Filip was in his sixties, a camp internee who had left Poland to settle in Israel. He made an unlikely ghoul, for he had been a rabbi, and a brilliant one, from what I had heard. But hatred had changed the course of his life, too. He was bald and jowly, his face spotted with age marks. His eyes were clear and blue, and he still had no need for glasses.

I tried to get up. My back was against a gravestone; the smell of the well-tended grass seemed to revive me.

"Just relax, you still look pale," Filip said. "You created quite a noise there, trying to grandstand the coroner." He smiled. "What happened to you?"

"Something I ate, I think. The heat. Old age."

"I've got ten years on you." He turned to look back at the grave site. The party was over; most everyone had left. "They took the bones to a laboratory," Filip said. "It looks like this is it."

"You think that was really Mengele?" I asked.

"It depends on what the forensic doctors have to say, but for my part, I think it's him. Once the Germans got hold of Mengele's letters, it was all over. Did you see the couple standing beside the police chief? Wolf and Liselotte Bossert. They took care of Mengele; he was at their beach house when he died. The police found his letters and personal objects at their home in the city, along with a book he'd written."

I knew most of this. "The Germans really gave you a screwing, didn't they?"

"Both us and the Americans; this was supposed to be a joint venture. But the Germans conveniently forgot to notify any of us. They just dispatched some of their LKA people down here and flushed it all out.

We heard about it when you did, probably; after it was leaked, so the Germans would get the right publicity. But what can you expect from Germans?" Although he was joking, there was a harshness in his voice. He meant it. "Are you feeling better now?"

I stood up, testing. "I feel fine," I said, although my stomach still hurt. We walked back to the exhumed grave. They had taken everything, every bit of wood from the casket. The gravediggers were standing about, as if admiring the hole they had dug, and then, reluctantly, they began to shovel back the dirt.

"I understand you're living in America," Filip said.

I nodded.

"And teaching at university. Why did you leave Israel?"

"I guess I became tired of it all," I said.

"What do you mean?"

"I wanted to leave the war behind, I wanted to forget."

"But you're here."

I sighed and looked out over the cemetery at the hundreds of odd angled and weathered headstones, which were like concrete sentences punctuated with the marble and stone crypts and mausoleums of the wealthy. The grass was cut so short it might be used as turf for a golf course, and the sun bleached the gravestones white as bones in a desert. But Mengele's bones...they were brown, as brown as the water of the Amazon, as brown as the cafuzos who had dug them up. Mengele wouldn't like that, for surely his bones should be Aryan white. Or so it would seem.

"You said that Mengele had written a book. Have you seen it?" I asked.

"No," Filip said. "But I understand it was an auto-biography. He called it *Fiat Lux...Let There Be Light.*"

CHAPTER TWO
WILD FIRE

The pain in my stomach was not from bad food, but from bowel cancer. I checked myself into a hospital in São Paulo, where they gave me a private room overlooking a low, flat roof that seemed to exist solely to provide a surface for the television antennae that grew out of the tar like steel plants. In the distance were gray buildings, brick chimneys, and the miasma of pollution that seemed to soften everything in this city...a city I had always hated. I had a small ranch near the gigantic King Ranch, which is in Amazon country just outside of Belém, and I wanted nothing more than to return there and let Onca, a heavy Indian woman of Yąnomamö extraction whom I had hired to take care of the place, look after me. But afraid as I was—and I was terrified—I couldn't bring myself to return to the States. It was as if I'd never had a life there, as if only the ranch felt like home; and I wanted to forget the university and my whole life in upstate New York. The ranch was the only place I'd ever felt completely comfortable, perhaps because it was so isolated, for even now, forty years later, I associated the steel and concrete of civilization with the camps. I could live and work and teach in cities, but the little boy that still lived inside me could only sleep in the red-tiled stucco house outside of Belém.

I endured the batteries of tests, the stool samples and barium enemas, the GI series and colonoscopies. As if to further complicate matters, I developed an ugly blister on my right cheek, just below where my glasses touch. Then another appeared on my mouth and scalp, and on my chest. The lesions wept a clear liquid; the one in my mouth left a constant bitter taste. My doctor, a no-nonsense woman who wore her long, beautiful black hair in a bun, explained that I had also developed a form of pemphigus, called *wild fire*, which was found only in certain areas of Brazil. Pemphigus was also a disease that middle-aged Jews were susceptible to. It was a virulent condition, and the usual cure was cortico-steroids and antibiotic therapy. But the corticosteroids might increase the growth of the spreading cancer. She would try 75 mg of a drug called Methotrexate.

Still, the wild fire was minor in comparison with the cancer. If I would take chemotherapy and radia-tion treatments for the cancer, she could give me six months to a year longer to live.

But I would probably need a bowel operation.

And I would have to wear a colostomy bag around on my stomach.

No, I thought. I wasn't going to live in hospital to gain a few months of pain. I wasn't going to die to the smell of antisepsis and live in the white rooms near the laboratories. Laboratories.... I could see Mengele's laboratory in my mind as if I had just left it.

Even as the doctor talked to me, I distanced myself from her and her words. I was numb, in shock, I supposed, and it was like being inside a cool, wet cloud high above the ground. I knew that I would be making a long fall any second now, yet it was as if fear and death and all the other emotions had become mere intellectual states. I considered my own death as if it was someone else's. Perhaps because I *couldn't* bring myself to believe any of it.

I suddenly began to tremble.

I stared out the window at the wild sculpture of rooftop antennae below and could think only of Mengele—Uncle Pepi, who had said that my twin brother and I wouldn't be in hospital for long. I grimaced, for the sonovabitch had been telling the truth. He had intended on killing both of us. But I had had one up on him. He hadn't gotten me. He had tried, but he had failed. Or had he...?

Irrational as it was, I found myself blaming Mengele for the cancer and the lesions. I couldn't help but feel that they were a parting gift from him. As I had looked into the hollows of his skull—I, who was alive and he, who was dead—*he* had somehow magically transformed my lunch of tainted food into cancer; and like Job's wife, who had taken that one last look back at Sodom, the place of her youth, I had looked into the dark shadows that had once been Mengele's blue eyes, and he opened up my skin and made it bubble, as if his death's-head's stare was invisible fire scorching my flesh.

I knew then that I was going home...to Belém, back to the ranch. I would die properly. In my own home.

And I would still have one up on Mengele.

* * * * * * *

My *fazenda* was small, barely four hundred hectares, while the other neighboring ranches were paced out at several hundreds of thousands of hectares. My manager Genaro, who had been a *macheteiro*, a drifter, drove me home from Belém in my 'pickoppy'. He was in his sixties, of white and Indian extraction. I knew very little about him, except that he was born near Manaus on the Rio Negro; he was quiet and looked sullen, perhaps because his lower jaw jutted out, but his pale blue eyes revealed an intelligence that seemed to be belied by his habit of reclining wherever and whenever possible. He was tall, thin and wiry, extremely well-muscled for a man his age. He had high cheekbones and black hair greased back away from his high forehead. His left cheek was distended from a roll of tobacco; his front teeth were missing. Yet for all that he was a formidable-looking man. He reminded me of a condor, or some other great, ungainly bird.

We drove down the Belém-Brasilia highway, which was like driving through hell, for much of the land to either side was on fire, and in some places the flames reached toward the cracked red ground along the highway. The sky was dark with smoke. The acrid smell was overwhelming, and the heat came in waves that seemed to suck away every bit of moisture. What wasn't burning was as scorched and dry as a desert; the burned stumps of trees reached out like props in a Grade B horror movie. All the jungle hereabouts would soon be converted into grassland, which the soil could support for five years at best. Most jungle soil is less than three inches deep. Burn down the trees and the microorganisms that feed minerals back into the soil die. Then the rain erodes the soil. The soil becomes sand. And what's left is red hardpan: laterite. Then more jungle has to be burned to produce more farm and pasture land.

But the worst of the conflagration was over; the land had been burning for some time. I had seen firestorms in this part of the country where clouds would form over the trees and rain would fall in sheets. Lightning would snake into the trees and as one looked into the isolate darkness, it seemed as if the last days promised in the bible had finally come. I felt a pang of guilt, for my little ranch had also been burned out of the jungle, but I had used the land wisely, had not extended myself, and was determined not to cut into any more of the jungle. The jungle was like a womb for me. I could afford to sell the cattle and just live on the *fazenda*.

It was a moot point. I would be long gone before the soil lost its nutrients and died.

We stopped in the town of Paragominas for gas. A small, dusty town square, dirty pastel buildings, sand demons boiling into life with every gust of wind, a few bars with pickups parked in front, the sounds of loud *carimbo* music and laughter, a young man wearing cowboy boots and a Stetson hat leading a donkey loaded with leather bags down the main street. I had taken a pill for the pain in my stomach, and although I knew the ache was still there, I felt removed from it. The nausea remained, however. I could not yet believe it was real, that I was going to die. For as much death as I had seen during my life, now, when it was once again upon me, I refused it. I was more mature, more willing to accept life's grim realities, when I was ten years old and part of Mengele's zoo. I ground my teeth, a habit that my ex-wife had always complained about, and once again I began to tremble. It was already dark and rather than stay in what looked more like a ghost-town in the American northwest than a village in the jungle, I insisted that we drive on. Genaro would have probably liked to stay at least long enough to play some pool in the bars and drink a few fingers of *cachaça*— Brazilian white rum.

Even in the darkness, I could feel when we were once again deep into jungle. The air was stifling, wet as a warm bath; my eyes stung and sweat rolled under my shirt, down my armpits, chilly in evaporation. A Culex mosquito flew into the cab of the pickup and its high-pitched whine almost drove me crazy until I finally managed to swat it.

"We are almost home, Meester," Genaro said at dawn, as the shadows that were hundred feet tall trees on either side of the road turned glaucous green and then finally came to life as a universe of viridescence, all the possibilities of green—celdadon, bice, emerald, beryl, aquamarine, olive green, evergreen, blue green, leek green, yew green, serpentine green, variscite green, turquoise green, mignonette, milori, chromium, terra verde, reseda—towering walls of trees and vines and air plants and ferns. I took another pill, which I had difficulty swallowing without water, and nodded. We had not talked for the entire trip; it was unusual that he would say anything at all without prompting.

"Is everything okay at the *fazenda*?" I asked, feeling the need for company in the wet grayness of morning. I felt lost, swallowed.

But Genaro didn't answer, which meant that indeed everything was okay or he would have told me what was wrong. Finally, after what seemed like a long time of concentration for him, Genaro said in a slow, tight voice, as if it was very difficult for him to speak, "I know you are dying."

"What?" I asked, shocked.

But Genaro didn't answer.

"You must speak now," I said, sitting forward, leaning toward him, as if he were going to whisper to me how he had found out.

His face tightened. "I knew you were dying before you left. Onca told me this. She also told me to tell you not to be afraid."

Onca, who took care of the house for me, was his wife. Once when I had asked her why someone who was so happy and talkative and full of life would choose someone as serious and quiet as Genaro for a husband, she laughed and said, "I'm a *bruxa*, you know what that is? Surely you have heard of *macumba* and *espiritisme*. Yes?" I had; they were indigenous religions that worshiped and, if one believed, used spirits. They used good spirits to protect themselves from bad spirits and were not above calling on foreign spirits for help, spirits such as Yara, which was supposed to be an American Indian, or white spirits such as Maria Lunga or Pai Jacobi, which could sometimes be used to harm people or accomplish evil ends. "Well," she continued, "I can see things. And Genaro helps me to do that. Sometimes I think *he's* a spirit." She laughed, as if she thought I would believe that bruxas were just part of the natural weave of things. And in some way I suppose I did, for I still couldn't separate the nightmare of my time in the camps from the reality. As I remembered Mengele, seeing him that first time, I could believe he was a spirit, a demon brought into the world; and even now, I remembered him as the man who was father, god, and tormentor. I remembered the feel of his clean-shaven face as he lifted me up once when he was in a good mood; and yet he had somehow merged with his death, and that fleshy monster had become skeletal in my mind; his face became that hollow-socketed skull the coroner had held high in Embu. And in my mind he was alive and dead, a grisly memory of the reality of sweet Onca's spirit world.

Genaro wouldn't talk at all for the rest of the trip. He kept his eyes straight ahead, and we finally came to the open gate of the Fazenda, then down my road to the driveway. The red tile roof of the arcaded porches glowed wetly in the sun and I felt better just seeing the gardens and the white stucco walls stained with rust and dirt. I felt suddenly sleepy.

The next thing I remembered was waking up in my room.

* * * * * * *

The sun poured through my bedroom window and I could hear the familiar screams of the pia, a small gray bird that the Indians called *dai-a-pior*, which meant 'worse to come.' The bird would softly whistle and then would break out in staccato-like shrieks. I couldn't stand the screeing, but like the terrible and unearthly screams of the howler monkeys, it was comforting if only because it was familiar.

"Well, Meester finally wakes up," Onca said, bringing me breakfast of milk, juice, a starchy gruel, and ice cream. Not her usual breakfast fare, nor mine. I discovered another lesion on my neck, which I would not allow myself to touch, lest it spread. I had to take my medication, I told myself, aware of the irony that here I was dying and yet I was concerned with a skin disease. But the taste of the sore in my mouth, and the constant awareness that there were others all over my body repulsed me, as if the pemphigus was an external sign of what was happening inside of me. But Onca only laughed and said, "You look like a young boy who hasn't yet found a woman."

"What?" I asked.

"You know, you're getting pimples. They'll go away once you start using your thing again like a man." She giggled and her wide face that in repose could appear as sullen as Genaro's seemed to partake completely of her smile. She tilted her head back as she looked at me, a habit of hers. Her mouth curled downward, which gave her an expression that was almost French. Her dark complexion was flawless, smooth as pond water, but her face seemed flattened. She wore a very faded dress that was cut much to short for her; it revealed her heavy legs and thighs and the outlines of her large breasts, which had nurtured seven children. Four of them died, she had said; the others grew up.

"Do you talk to Genaro like that?" I asked.

"Much worse, Meester. Much worse." She put the tray on my lap and said, "Eat, you'll feel better."

"What the hell is it?" I asked. The last thing I wanted was food; the very thought of eating made me queasy.

"Do you want me to feed you?" she asked.

"Don't talk to me that way," I snapped. "I can't eat... but you can tell me what it is."

"It's made from the manioc, which I mashed up and add some things."

"What other things?"

"Some *carapanauba* bark, a little *paxuri* seeds, and *cachaça*, and maybe something else, I maybe forget. You know what they are?"

"*Cachaça* I know, but the rest...I'm not eating—"

Try it, you'll see. I promise it won't hurt you. Would

I be stupid enough to kill the golden fleece?"

I couldn't help but smile. Over the years I had always read to her once or twice a week, for she didn't know how to read, nor would she learn. But she loved fairy tales, and I tried to bring back new books to read her. Those stories would turn her into a child, an odd and wonderful thing to watch, for to me at least she seemed like the embodiment of the earth mother. She even looked like the prehistoric statues archaeologists had found all over the world; they were small, but had overdeveloped breasts and large stomachs. She was somehow natural, idiosyncratic, and universal.

"It's goose, not fleece," I said, and, giving in, I took a spoonful of the glassy-looking gruel; it had no taste at all, but then my mouth became numb, as if the mush had been spiked with Novocain. I could feel it numb my throat and more as the stuff worked its way down my esophagus to my stomach. There was a dish popular in Belém called *pato no tucupi*, which was famous for numbing the mouth. She must have used some of the same ingredients.

"Try some more," she insisted. "It will help your stomach. It will make the pain go away for a while."

But I couldn't keep the food from trickling out of the side of my mouth. "What's the ice cream for?" I asked.

"It makes the herbs work better."

That was true. As the ice-cream went down, I felt as if my insides were being air-conditioned, as if there were great cold places where my throat and chest and stomach had been, and I felt muzzy and light-headed, as if everything was slowly floating around me. "Genaro told me you knew I was dying," I said.

"I told him that."

"How did you know?"

"I had a dream about it when Genaro was making love to me. Sometimes I dream then. Often I do."

I felt myself blushing as she told me that, although I've never been a prude. Yet I felt embarrassed and chilled that she should see my death as she made love to her silent husband. I stared out the window at the neatly tended garden of jungle flowers and the evergreen trees that were in lavender bloom, but the white sash window-bars wavered and went out of focus. I did not feel pain in my stomach, only coolness. Now I imagined that dry breezes were passing though me. Onca must have used more than herbs in the gruel; I hoped it wasn't anything hallucinogenic. Probably not, I could trust her.

But she had put *something* in there....

I didn't want to ask her any more questions, yet I couldn't help myself; and she was standing before me, waiting, knowing that I would ask, and prepared to answer, as if she had dreamed this, too. Perhaps she had.

"What about your dream?" I asked. "Tell me about it."

"I dreamed about you and Genaro. Maybe because I was trying to make babies with Genaro. Sometimes dreams and truth get mixed up for me and I can't pull out one part from another. Do you understand?"

I didn't, but I nodded.

"And your dream?"

She turned toward the window and looked out. She seemed to be looking past the trees and gardens and yard and miles of pastureland that was as level as Iowa grassland. Deep in the distance was the rainforest, the real ruler of this land. "It was a good dream, but it wasn't good to dream it. You were with my Genaro in a boat. He was driving this boat. You sat in the front, but you were your own dream and it was a terrible dream. You were bones without flesh, yet you weren't dead; and your bones were the color as the water. Brown as mud, just like the Amazonas. And Genaro was taking you to meet death so you could get yourself back." She shivered and made a gesture in the air. "He told me he would do that for you."

"What do you mean?" I asked, my words slurred from the Novocain-like herb she had put in the food. "Do *what* for me?"

"I feel close to you, Meester, but I told him not to do this, but he believes it is a matter of honor."

"You're not making sense," I said, frustrated with all this mumbo-jumbo.

"He will take you to meet your death so you may live. That is what *your* dream told me when I had my dream. Dreams come from people, but they can be alive on their own, to talk to each other, just like people."

"Onca, how you found out about my disease, I don't know. I'll give you that. But you—"

"We know someone who can help you," Onca said.

"If I wouldn't go to hospital to have them radiate me and do everything else, I certainly wouldn't go to a witch doctor. But I thank you, I appreciate your concern."

"This person isn't a witch doctor, Meester."

"Than what is he?"

"He's a white man. A doctor. You know him, I think."

"Who?"

"That's all I have from the dream," she said. "Maybe later I will have more. Then maybe you will be ready." With that she took the tray, leaving me only the milk on my bed stand, and left the room.

"Onca," I shouted, but she didn't—and I knew she wouldn't—come back. The image that had formed in my mind was, of course, that of Mengele. Death. But that was impossible, and yet I still felt the hackles raise on my back, cold as the scales of a fish.

* * * * * * *

That night I was awakened by a sharp scream. My first thought was of howler monkeys, but the shriek was of too short a duration, and sounded too human.

It was Onca.

CHAPTER THREE
DRY STORM

In the days that followed, I would get out of bed early and wander around the ranch. I couldn't stand to sleep. I would wake up screaming and sweaty, but I would be unable to remember my nightmares. I hated the onset of darkness, and when I finally retired to my room, I would read until I couldn't stay awake any longer. I ate what Onca gave me and, although my mouth was continually numb, I had stopped taking the pills. I was living day to day, and the days seemed interminably long, as if I was a child and once again had time to be bored. But I wasn't impatient. I didn't think about dying hardly at all, and the lesions on my body had begun to clear up with the medicine. Onca also insisted I wash with a putrid smelling brown herb she placed in a glass by my washbasin every day. It looked like a turd and was as slippery and hard as a wet stone.

But I felt safe for the time being, as if I could live in this eternal present until I was ready to face what was happening to me...until I could face dying. I became an ice-cream junkie, mildly high all day, buzzing with cool, inconsequential thoughts, slurring my words as if I had just left the dentist's chair, and feeling as if my insides were cold as a refrigerator, even while I was sweating in the tropical humidity.

Genaro introduced me to the new men, who weren't happy to discover that their *empreteiro* was going to be here permanently. Genaro had unusual luck keeping fieldhands, for most *macheteiros* won't work longer than thirty days before moving on. It was obvious that they respected him and considered him their boss; I was simply an intruder. I wondered if my presence would make them insecure enough to leave.

He asked my advice on various things, such as what to do with the grass we'd been experimenting with: a type of grass that could be planted again and again without depleting the soil of nutrients. But the grass would often turn brown and die, even when there was sufficient rain. Some years ago I had also had the idea of trying to crossbreed the indigenous humpback zebu with American stock. The zebu is perfectly adapted to the Amazonian climate and is extraordinarily hardy, but its meat, unfortunately, tastes like old shoes. One afternoon I watched Genaro artificially inseminate several cows with large syringes of bull's sperm. He wore a long green plastic glove and grimaced every time he did it. But so far we had had no luck in producing a viable crossbreed.

Genaro was patient and dutifully showed me all work that was being done on the ranch. But more often than not my concentration would wander, and I would go off by myself. I suspect Genaro was happy to be on his own.

I began to lose weight. Every day I shed a few pounds; every day Onca would insist I eat more. But I had no appetite, except for ice cream. I began staying in my room more often, as the pain in my stomach became harder to muffle.

And then it stopped raining.

Days on end without even a drizzle, an eerie phenomenon in a rain-forest. Genaro told me that he had known of this happening before; once, when he had been a *macheteiro* in the Araguaia Valley, it did not rain for two hundred days. If this occurred here, we would be out of business. Although I knew it was wrong thinking, for I had responsibilities to the others on the ranch, I could not help but think that it would be a fitting end to it all. It was as if nature was in league with my death to have my world fall with me. I remembered a quote from the Talmud, something to the effect that every man is a whole universe to himself, which is irrevocably lost when he dies. This seemed like an omen, a physical extension of my death.

But although there was no rain, dry storms occurred several times a day. The sky would turn black, clouds would boil, thunder would crash like cars on a freeway after explosions of lightning, yet no rain. It was disconcerting. I would pace the room during the storms, agitated, listening to the wind breathing around the house, until finally I would have to go outside, for I felt trapped, as if the thick stucco walls were imperceptibly getting closer, as if the electricity of the storm was depleting my room of oxygen and leaving only a hint of ozone to burn in my nose.

It was an odd sensation walking through the fields in the stormy darkness, in the chill of imminent downpour; and yet during those times the air would be as dry as a fall day in upstate New York. The storms seemed to bring out the insects, clouds of them buzzing around my face, a constant annoyance. In a grove of huge Brazil nut trees a green parrot screamed, as if frightened. I could smell the moulds and sweet damp aroma of decay that I associated with forest floor as I passed the grove. But my mind was still blank, emptied, and I seemed to float above the jagged teeth of reflection and memory.

And then I found one of Genaro's *macheteiros* dead in the south pasture. Thirty head of steer had fallen around him, their tongues black and hanging out of their mouths, their eyes bulging. I stopped and stood there, realizing an instant later that I had been holding my breath. I could hear the roll of thunder and the buzzing of hundreds of flies.

The ranch hand had fallen face down on the ground. I pulled him over, grasping his arm, and shuddered when I discovered that he was covered with maggots. They were crawling all over his face, in and out of his mouth, and over his eyes, which were wide open, as if he were surprised to find himself in such a state.

It looked as if someone had tossed a grenade into the area. The *macheteiro* and the cattle he was tending must have been hit by lightning.

CHAPTER FOUR
MACHETEIRO DREAMS

That night I dreamed about the *macheteiro*. But in my dream the man was transformed into David, my brother.

I was back in Auschwitz, which was like a park filled with great trees in tended rows, and birds were screeing all around me as animals crashed through nearby bushes. Yet I wasn't afraid, for this place was a concentration of life rather than death. I walked toward a building that looked like my house on the ranch, except this one was made of red brick and had a huge chimney. I opened the door and saw David strapped into an electrical apparatus of the kind Mengele used to use on us in Auschwitz. Then I saw Mengele. He was older and looked grandfatherly.

As soon as he saw me, he nodded and gave the order to send electrical shocks through David until he died.

I ran across the room to my brother and tried to unfasten the leather bands that held him against the machine, but as I touched him his skin turned black under my hands, his flesh became like parchment and broke off in pieces, and his eyes that were watching me, imploring, exploded, washing me with tears and membrane.

I screamed, and Mengele consoled me, shushing me like a baby, and I could smell the odor of cigarettes on his breath and the strong soap he used. Then he ordered the experiment to be reversed, and as if I had been watching a film being rewound, my brother came back to life, his skin healed, and his eyes, which were as intelligent and questioning as they had ever been, were welling with tears as he said my name. I turned to thank Uncle Pepi, Mengele. He accepted my thanks and then ordered one of his men to tie *me* to the machine. I begged him not to do this, and just as he was about to lower his hand—the signal to turn on the electricity—I begged him to take my brother instead of me.

He smiled, and brought his hand down smartly.

I could hear the thrum of the generator, and I knew I was going to die. But it wasn't me who felt the heart-stopping shock of electricity.

It was David.

It was the *macheteiro*.

His skin turned black and then to ash.

* * * * * * *

I woke up in the darkness of my bedroom and called Onca, as if I were a child who had had a bad dream and needed his mother. The pain in my stomach was a throbbing; I imagined it as a bright light inside me; I imagined it as electrical wires touching, sending electrical jolts of pain through me, frying me from the inside out. But the pain, and the dream, had sensitized me. I had questions and wanted answers instead of herbs.

And I remembered the dreams I had been having for the past week.

I had had this dream of David and Mengele, over and over.

It was as if I had dreamed the reality of the *macheteiro*. As if *I* had murdered him. Just as I had murdered David. Just as I was murdering myself.

But I had also had another recurring dream...Onca's dream of being on the river with Genaro.

* * * * * * *

"Yes, Meester," Onca said as she stood in the darkness of my room. She was like a shadow, a disembodied voice. I reached over to the bedstead and switched on the lamp. "Ouch," she said, shielding her eyes. She wore a flower-patterned housedress that she held tightly around herself, as if I had somehow called her in here to catch a glimpse of her naked flesh.

"I'm sorry," I said, embarrassed. "I had a bad dream," but as I looked into her face I remembered something that I had blocked out of my memory for all these years. I saw her brown eyes, wide as a child's, and remembered being sent on an errand when I was a child in the camp—the nature of the errand, I could not remember. I had gotten lost. I was frightened, for if I were found walking about by the wrong person, I might be turned to smoke in the crematorium the next day. (Hadn't hundreds of children, most of them my own age, been sent to the crematoriums just because they weren't tall enough? I remembered when that happened: It was Yom Kippur, and I had to put stones in my shoes in order to gain a centimeter.) I passed by a door and opened it, hoping it was the office where I had been sent. But the room was empty, nothing but two long tables and high-backed wooden chairs. A high window covered with mesh let in a wan gray light. None of the ceiling lamps were turned on. But the far wall was covered with a taut white canvass, and attached to it with pins were eyes of every color. It was as if they were all staring at me. Condemning me for having arms and legs and a head, while they were dead. Forever staring outward onto one of Mengele's bare walls.

"Do you wish me to get you something?" Onca asked.

"No," I said, "but I want to know about your dream." She looked uncomfortable, for she turned her head away; it was a subtle movement, but I had come to know her enough to understand her body language. "I've been dreaming about being on a boat with Genaro, too. What do you know about this doctor?"

She shrugged and sat down in a chair near the bed, her back to the window. I had pulled the mosquito netting away, draping it behind the head post. "This you must ask Genaro."

"But I'm asking you first. Then if I decide to pursue it further, I can talk to Genaro. But he can be difficult to talk to, and there are some things I need to know."

"Okay, if I know something I will tell you." She pulled her housedress around her, a nervous habit.

"In this dream you had about me, you said you knew about a doctor who could make me well. Was that your dream or is it true that you know about a doctor?"

"It is both. I had the dream, and I know about a doctor."

"Who is he?" I asked. "Where is he from?"

She shook her head. "Genaro met this man a long time ago. He only told me so after my dream."

"What did he tell you?"

"Genaro does not talk so easily, as you know that. But Genaro was very sick. The man helped him."

"Any doctor might have been able to do that?" I said.

"He had *febre*. It had killed everyone where he was."

"Where was that?"

She shrugged. "He says above Manaus in Aika territory."

The Aika were an Indian tribe, part of the Yąnomamö, the largest primitive group in the Amazon. Onca was Yąnomamö. Perhaps Genaro was too.

"Were you with him then?" I asked."

"I told you, no. It happened before I knew him. What I know is from him and from the dream, that's all, Meester, I swear that."

"How did Genaro get out to see this doctor when the others didn't, when the others died."

"You have to ask him these things," she said impatiently. She looked tired. Her eyes were swollen, but

I had noticed that they've been like that for the past few days. "Genaro says this man is powerful like a sorcerer."

"And what makes you think I would know this man?" I asked.

"I had the dream, which told me that. That's how I know. I had the dream before Genaro told me about what happened to him. That's how I know. The dream said this man could save you. Some of that was told to me by your own dream, I think." As she talked, she became more agitated and upset. "You don't want to try it, that's okay, too. Everybody dies anyway, and if you go you'll pay for it anyway. So will Genaro."

"What do you mean?"

"Just that. I don't know. The fuck if I know," and she turned her head away again, this time not so subtly.

"The whole thing is crazy," I said. "It's crazy that I would even consider talking about it."

"Yes," she said. "Crazy. Now I think I should be sleeping." She stood up and walked to the door.

"Onca?"

"Yes, Meester?" Her bulk filled up the doorway, part of her in deep shadow like some great ship about to break away from its moorings.

"A few nights ago I heard you scream."

She stared at me.

"Why did you scream? Do you remember?"

"I remember."

I didn't say anything more, but waited for her to go on, if she would.

"The scream was for Genaro, but for you too," Onca said. "I will tell you," and she walked back in the room, but kept her distance from me. "I dreamed about what happened to Genaro when he was cured by this doctor. I saw in this dream what Genaro was like before he saw this man. He was not so quiet, he had more life. And then he became like you...."

I felt her words, as if I had been kicked and the wind had gone out of me, but I said nothing.

"In the dream I saw my husband as he really is, I felt his thoughts, and I felt a sadness that took the life out of Genaro, that took his words and laughter and juice. I can't describe this sadness, but it was as if he felt he had done something terrible, even though he didn't, as if he carried terrible things that weren't his. Like you, Misteer. The same as you. And I feel afraid for both of you, because I know you are going back to meet this sorcerer, and I want to stop you. But I don't want you to die. But I don't want you to carry weight, and Genaro, he cannot carry any more. So I don't know. But if you go, Meester, you must take care of Genaro, no matter what. You must promise me this."

I nodded and saw that she was crying, although her voice never wavered, just increased in strength.

She left and I realized that she was right. I was going to go. I would only become bedridden if I stayed. If I was going to die, it might as well be in the open, on the Amazon, than here. And as I turned off the light, I thought about David and my mother—I had never known my father, for he had died in an automobile accident before I was born. I remembered snatches of childhood before the camp, and I felt the old anger and hatred for Mengele. I had spent the better part of my life tracking him, to balance the scales, and in those years I had lost the focus of anger; finding him had become my *raison d'être*, but it was a choir I had become resigned to. My passion was gone, walled deep inside, its only escape dreams and nightmares. But now, perhaps my fear of death rekindled it. If there was a doctor living in the jungle, I would find him. If, impossibly, he was Mengele, I would kill him.

I would kill him for David.

For my mother.

For me, for the life he had taken.

And if he were just a doctor, a missionary treating the Indians, perhaps he would help me to die well.

As I sank through layers of gray thought to sleep, I felt a strength leaching into my old bones. I dreamed that I held the knife to Mengele. I dreamed that Mengele never was, that I had a life, a family instead of a few ugly affairs. A family instead of an empty apartment. A family instead of a *fazenda* Indian woman who treated me as an child—perhaps out of love, perhaps because it was her character to mother.

But as I slept I found my anger and hatred once again. I seethed with it, I was overjoyed with it, and even in the deepest of dreams, I knew that if I were going to die, I would have a purpose. Even if Mengele was dead, even if he was the hollow-socketed skull held up by the coroner in Embu, I would find him, in life or in death.

For in my dream, I could see into Onca's dreams, into Genaro's dreams; and in deep sleep I believed in sorcery, for now I too was a sorcerer, a demon, and if it took a dream-journey for me to reach and exorcise my past, then so be it.

* * * * * *

The next day I talked with Genaro. We were in my dining room and Onca had prepared the table with silver and crystal as if this was to be my last supper. It was dusk, and the room took on a smoky appearance; the oriental rug that covered the rough plank hardwood floor gave a cozy warmth to the room, as did the hearth, for there were nights here when a fire was in order. "I can't just make plans to go into the jungle," I said. "I must know exactly where we're going."

Genaro nodded; he stood beside me and fidgeted while Onca brought a bottle of wine to the table. I had asked him to stay to supper, but he had awkwardly and politely declined. Under normal circumstances, he would have made himself comfortable in one of the plush chairs by the fireplace, as if it was he who owned the ranch and not me. But tonight he was different, taut, as if he were a soldier out on a dangerous maneuver. "We must get to Manaus," he said, "and then we'll go up Rio Branco. We can rent a 'motor.' Then we go north, right up river, almost to Venezuela, I think. Maybe *in* Venezuela. I don't know that. Wakatauteri country, not much on the maps. Dangerous."

"Why?" I asked.

"Some tribes still eating people. The Inambu and the Casao. I saw Inambu once." He shook his head slightly, which for Genaro connoted real disgust. And there is disease like black river *febre*, which kills you in a day. I know of this, too."

I nodded; we would be well armed; and I, at least, had little to lose as far as diseases went.

"But more than that, something hard to put into words."

"Try, Genaro."

He looked even more uncomfortable and kept glancing at Onca, giving her nasty looks, as if it were her fault entirely that he was called in to talk to me. "It's different up there from other jungle places," he said after a time. "More dreams."

"What?"

"Dreams, they are real, like us. You can see them. They are dangerous. They can look like animals, but they aren't. You will see them if you go. You think not, but you will. Your dreams, too, will be real."

I glanced at Onca, who would not make eye contact with me. She seemed to be hearing these things for the first time. This whole thing was crazy. I should lay down in my bed and die in my house, not be planning my last adventure, this field trip into superstition. But somehow I was committed, as if indeed the dreams were in some sense real.

"How long will it take us to get there?" I asked.

"From Manaus?"

I nodded.

"With a motor?"

I nodded again.

"Maybe three days, including the walking."

I groaned just thinking about that, for I was in constant pain now. It was a dull ache, even with Onca's herbs and the prescription drugs. But I continued on as if nothing was wrong, by sheer determination, for I knew that once I allowed myself to become bedridden, I would be finished. The pemphigus, which I had been treating with the methotrexate prescribed by my doctor, had responded somewhat to treatment; it did not clear up, but did not seem to get much worse. Onca, of course, firmly believed it was the soap she had given me; and when I stopped using the foul smelling stuff, I did, indeed, begin to break out. But I also broke out when I stopped using the prescription.

"Will you make me a list of what we'll need to take?" I asked.

He nodded.

"I'll take care of the plane and the motor," I said.

"The boat it's easier to work out when we get to Manaus. I know someone who will let us use his motor for fifty thousand cruzeiros."

That was about a hundred dollars.

"Do you really believe that this...doctor can help me?" I asked as he turned to leave.

"If he's still there," he said. "That is the chance you will take."

"Are you afraid?" I asked him.

But Genaro just looked at me, his face tight, his

eyes hard and glittering. I was reminded of the *mussel-manner* in the camp—those internees who had given up life, but were still alive. The walking dead. But in that instant when our eyes met, everything seemed to change.

I felt his fear like a spider crawling under my shirt.

I felt a connection with him.

I believed him.

CHAPTER FIVE
THE MAGIC OF DARKNESS

We left a week later and traveled light. I bought comfortable sneakers, much better in rain forest than combat or jungle boots, and stocked our first aid kit with extra medicine. I took cloroquine and Fansidar tablets, which would take care of all but the deadly strains of malaria, insect repellents, and various other medicines, including tablets to purify water, which was often tainted with feces. We also brought a few gifts to trade: cigarette lighters, two powerful flashlights, nails and needles, combs, a small tape recorder, cheap plastic watches, a few pairs of shorts and dresses, and a hammock. I took several wads of paper money, just to be safe, which I carried inside my shoe, in a money belt, and in my wallet.

And I also took a thirty-eight-caliber revolver.

We would fly first to Itaituba in an old Brazilian Bandeirante, which could hold fifteen passengers, and then on to Manaus. I had called an old friend who lived in Belém and ran a one-man commuter airline of sorts—actually, he was a glorified bush pilot. He made most of his money smuggling. He was an expert on gemstones, and he showed me three clearwater diamonds and a fist-sized amethyst crystal he was planning to sell. He had picked them up in Roraima from the *garimpeiros*, a rough lot, many with forged passports, who risked everything they owned to dig for the stones and perhaps become rich. The stones he bought from them were *brute*, or uncut, and he cut each one himself. He boasted that he was the finest lapidary in Brazil. Perhaps he was, for the stones, especially the diamonds, were beautiful, almost transparent, with a touch of blue; it was like holding cold pieces of the Brazilian sky. His name was Bob Pizor, and he was an American. He holstered a pistol on his hip and claimed that in Roraima and Porto Velho, where he did a lot of business, you needed a gun if you were going to survive. Yet Bob looked like the antitheses of an adventurer. He was tall and very thin. His shoulders were always hunched, as if he found being tall an embarrassment. He was balding, yet his hair seemed a patchwork flecked with gray. He wore black thick-framed plastic glasses and had uneven teeth that were so white they might have been caps. His full mustache exaggerated his thin face, which was an expanse of forehead, gaunt cheeks, and a cleft chin. He had been a salesman in Long Island. Airplanes were his hobby. He had a family, three children. And here he was in Brazil, enjoying himself hugely and complaining constantly of how guilty he felt about his misspent life. He was the most nervous and intense man I had ever met. He smoked four packs of cigarettes a day, drank too much, and never seemed to sleep. He also made a fetish of wearing a black suit and tie, as if he were still living in suburbia. But commuters in Sea Cliff, Long Island didn't wear revolvers.

He picked us up at a private airstrip on a nearby ranch, and we flew around storms, past the black thunderheads, and the plane shimmied and rattled and shook as if we were in an old bus. Below was rainforest, uniform, a seemingly endless sea of evergreen. It had often been described as an ocean, and that was the effect it had always had on me. Looking down through wisps of cloud, one was always on the verge of panic, for the forest seemed larger than life and somehow as deep and as dark as any uncharted undersea shelf. Genaro sat near a window, too, on the other side of me, and looked down. He was silent, and I imagined that he was feeling awe, just as I was. But Bob started talking, perhaps to break up the silence that seemed to be percolating up from the jungle floor below. "All this jungle used to scare the shit out of me. But I just stopped thinking about it, since I'm in the air all the goddamn time over it. If anything went wrong, though, we'd be shit out of luck. Even if we could survive crashing into the treetops, who the fuck would ever find us out here? I've known of planes going down; never found a one."

"What about your radio?" I asked.

Bob laughed. "Don't worry about it. This old horse feels like it's falling apart, but it's better than anything in its class, better than anything like it made in the USA." Without pause, he asked. "What are you doing with all that shit, anyway?" He meant our packs and provisions. " You still looking for war criminals?"

"No," I said, "just business."

Bob nodded, as if that would explain everything. "You still doing work for the *Post*?"

"Yes," I free-lance for them."

"You back here to work or just fucking the dog at your ranch?"

"A little of both," I said, feeling uncomfortable.

"And you're completely full of shit," he said. But he didn't ask anything more, and he never said a word about the pemphigus that disfigured my face.

We landed in Itaituba, and Bob said he wouldn't be more than a half-hour. We waited in the plane. I took a painkiller and watched planes taking off and landing, seemingly at once from opposite ends of the airstrip, for this was a gold-rush town, which might account for why Bob was making a stop.

Although Genaro was sitting right beside me, I felt absolutely alone, bereft. I had done nothing in my life but chase down a myth. Now, even when I knew that Mengele was dead, after I had *seen* his bones in the graveyard, I was still chasing the myth. Chasing it to death. I had no wife, no family. I shivered with the realization that I had suddenly leapt from all the possi-bilities of youth to the shock of mortality, as if the inter-vening wasted years had collapsed with the weight of my ennui, and here I was. Perhaps the stimulus had been seeing the jungle below me and trying to grasp its green infinities, and yet I felt I was slipping inescapably into its darkness. Even here in the noisy, gasoline-stinking afternoon, bright with sunlight, I knew that I had torn free of all that had been my life.

I felt as if I were back in the camps.

I was in pain. But that wasn't it. I was feeling the magic of darkness, of the underside of things, of slipping past the rational and the traditional...even though this was a scorching, transparently clear and bright afternoon. I had let the jungle take me, just as I had let Mengele take me. I was of one mind again, child and adult.

I looked away from the death-defying acrobatics of the pilots in the hundred or so planes taking-off and landing and found Genaro staring at me.

As if we were both *musselmanner.*

As if we were both lost.

Damned.

* * * * * * *

We were in Manaus by dusk. Bob had business to do in town and was going to stay the night. We took a taxi to a fleabag hotel we had both used over the years, a place just outside of the duty free zone. Manaus was probably one of the world's largest outdoor bazaars. The streets were filled with elegant turn-of-the-century buildings adorned with French ironware; below were shops selling electronic equipment, watches, cameras, stereos; and street vendors sold their wares on blankets laid out side by side on the baking sidewalks. Music of every variety was constant, and at night neon and prostitutes turned the area into a honky-tonk whorehouse. In the center of town were skyscrapers, for this hole in the jungle was also a place of international commerce. Further out were shack cities and the modern, middle-class subdivisions called *conjuntos*; and on the edge of town were the new factories, mostly Japanese, that assembled radios and televisions, for there was no import duty on components here. The stench of chemicals pervaded the air of Manaus; it was as if Trenton, New Jersey had been transplanted in Eden, in the primordial forest. From where we were we could just see the blue and gold tiles of the *Teatro do Amazonas* reflecting the tropical sun like a jeweled helmet; it wasn't a church, but an opera house built during the rubber boom.

Our hotel, *The Elegância*, had a charming old-world façade. It was four stories, stuccoed, and covered with creeping vine. Outside the door an old cabloco woman wearing very dirty clothes of very bright colors was selling parrots and wild animals in cages. The musky smell of jaguar was overpowering, even outside on the streets. There was a large male, just over five feet from nose to the root of his tail, in an inadequately small cage. It growled as we passed, a low vibration. I turned to look back, and it met my eyes. It was orange-tan with rosettes of black all over its body. It pressed its head against the bars, as if it could somehow slip past them through stealth alone.

What better guide to death than this cat by my door...?

We checked in, walked up two flights to three adjoining rooms. I felt tired and depressed. The room didn't help my mood: cracked plaster on walls and ceiling, a bed with a white cover that looked grimy and yellowed, and there was no door separating bedroom from bathroom. But my window overlooked the streets and I opened it fully. The sounds below were faint and muffled, yet comforting.

I cleaned myself up and lay down on the bed.

There was a knock on the door. I said "Enter" and Bob walked in with a bottle of *cachaça* and two water glasses.

"You still drink this stuff?" he asked, sitting down on the bed beside me.

"No, I haven't had a drink in some time."

"Well, here," he said, handing me a glass of the transparent liquid. "I got a big deal going down tomorrow. I'm nervous."

"What is it?" I asked.

"Gonna sell the stones, and some stuff I picked up in Itaituba. Then I'm going back home."

"What? I thought you loved it here."

"Time to go home," he said, pouring himself some more rum and then putting the bottle on the floor between his feet. "This is going to be a big shot for me, and I'm going to take the money and go back to the US of A. I talked to Tonie." Tonie was his wife.

"You mean she's going to take you back, after all these years?" I asked, incredulous.

"I've been writing her letters for the past year, and

calling her, you know, begging her forgiveness. The real problem's going to be with my kids. They're teenagers, and from what Tonie says, they hate my guts."

"You can work all that out," I said. "But I must admit, it's a surprise. It became dark quickly and the room glowed in blinking neon light from the barras below.

"I'll get a job. I gotta do something. But we'll have enough money, and I'll try to make it up to her. She thought I was dead, did you know that?" He laughed. "And when I called her the first time, she couldn't believe it was me, that I was down here, doing what I'm doing. I think now she's got some respect for me, you know what I mean? But, you know, she wasn't seeing anybody else. Christ, it's been ten years. It was as if she was waiting for me or something."

I nodded.

"So this is probably the last time we'll see each other for a while...if at all. We should have a party or something. So now you want to tell me what's going on with you?"

"There's nothing going on," I insisted.

"You're sick, and you smell bad. Tell me. I got a bad feeling about you, like you're dying or something. That's it, isn't it. You're dying. But what the fuck would you be doing out here, and don't give me any of that secret mission shit. You owe me at least an explanation. You still owe me one for that tip on that SS guy who you found in Uruguay. What happened to him?"

"He's dead."

"Who killed him?"

I didn't say anything; I didn't have to. We killed him in 1965. We were under orders from Mossad. He had been one of the executioners in Riga. I had bludgeoned him to death, and we put him in a trunk in Colombia Street near Carrasco. But killing him haunted me for years. I saw Mengele laughing at me as I hit the fugitive Nazi SS officer. Mengele supervised my dreams from that time on, for in that instant, I had become like him. I had become like the man who had killed my family. I had become the man I killed.

"Well," Bob said, "be seeing you." He picked up his bottle and stood up.

And then I told him that I was dying and going to see a witch doctor.

But I didn't tell him that he might, impossibly, be Mengele.

Bob stood by the bed, shoulders hunched, and looked at me. "Well, if the doctors can't help you, what the fuck else are you going to do? It makes as much sense as anything else. Wasn't there some guy that was in the news some years ago, a healer who operated without instruments? Maybe that was in Mexico, I can't remember." He suddenly stopped talking, as if he had embarrassed himself. Perhaps he thought that I was delusional, yet he had been taken in, just for an instant, only because he could believe that I was very ill.

He left the room, unable to say very much, unable to look straight at me, it seemed; but returned an hour later with three women.

"What the hell is this?" I asked.

"One last party, remember?" Then he knocked on Genaro's door, shouting, "Hey, Genaro, I bought you a present, open up."

The women huddled just inside the doorway. They were obviously prostitutes, overly made-up and wearing very tight, low-cut dresses and high spiked heels. The one standing closest to the door was of average height, and her hair was blond. She was pretty, but much too thin and flat-chested for my taste, and she had buck teeth, just slightly bucked, but enough to cause her to open her mouth slightly, which gave her a breathy look, a caricature of a nineteen fifties pin-up. The others had dark hair and looked like *caboclos*: part white and part Indian. Their features were sharp and thick and strong, as if created by a woodcutter rather than an etcher; their bodies, although shapely, were compact, as if they were made of denser stuff than the other woman. The *cabloclo* women were quite pretty. Both were tall and had long straight black hair that was so shiny as to have been oiled; one of them had a hairline scar on her cheek, which added to her feral appearance. But all of them looked hard and bored, and angry that they had to be here at all, that they would have to lay down under Bob or me or someone else in a foulsmelling bed and be pounded and suffocated for those few minutes that it took to come.

Well, they wouldn't have to worry about me. "Goddammit, Bob," I said as he returned to my room. "Get these people out of here."

"Don't you like them?" he asked.

"Just get them out."

"Okay," he said. "I paid for them, I'll take care of them. Your friend Genaro wouldn't answer his door."

"He probably knew what you were up to."

"That's such a crime?"

"I thought you were going back to your wife?"

"Not right away," he said grinning, looking like a mortician in a black suit with shiny pants.

I closed the door after them and was left once more to the almost hypnotic movement of light in the room. A red haze seemed to be blinking on and off, but it was dim, almost one with the dark. The neon out the window seemed to be reflections of the colors of my nightmares, and in the shifting shadows of the room I could almost imagine that Mengele was here, lowering his hand, giving the signal to electrocute my brother. I shivered with the same fear I had always had of being alone in the dark. I couldn't take a shower at night, for whenever I would close my eyes so as not to be stung by the soap, I would imagine that someone would be on the other side of the curtain, ready to grab me for another experiment. I switched on the lamp by the bed, carving out a dimly lit and isolated area of safety. I sat on the bed and listened to my past, the whisperings of boyhood thoughts; and I was afraid to close my eyes, lest I might see myself once more in the camp, lest I might see my brother screaming and then jerk bolt stiff at the shock of electricity; but there was more that I didn't want to see, that I was afraid to see. I was afraid to remember, to visualize, the look on the old man as I struck him. The SS officer, the killer of Riga, looked as if he was being eaten away by cancer; he must have weighed a hundred pounds. And as I killed him, he whispered 'mother.'

I didn't hear it until years later.

I heard it in recurring dreams, and it was my voice.

I rose from the bed and hurried to the door. "Bob," I shouted. "Bob...."

Genaro looked out from his room, and then he closed his door without a word.

Regretting my sudden change of mind, I went back into my room. Immediately there was a soft knock at the door. It was the woman with the scar. I let her into the room and turned off the lamp. She undressed in the neon, which was like firelight. She stared at me, taking off her blouse and her bra, and I felt frozen, an adolescent with his first whore. I undressed quickly, clumsily, while she watched, but I wouldn't remove my underclothes until I was under the sheet, for I didn't want her to see the marks of my pemphigus. Her touch was cool, her fingers surprising long, and I closed my eyes while she traced her nails over my chest and stomach, stopping short of my groin, a professional opening to her well-rehearsed act. Her face was tinged with red, softened somewhat by the outside light, and I held her face while she touched me, barely able to see her hairline scar that ran across her check. I kissed her, smelling cigarettes and perfume, and tasted the sugary residue of soda-pop, while she expertly took me inside her. This was going to be my last, I thought; and I was free, as if death was freeing me from disease and destination; but that too was illusion, for I was racing death as surely as I was pumping into this woman's body; and destination was now destiny.

Mengele.

Even now, even here...especially now.

The woman was quiet, her breathing even, It was as if she were in another room entirely, removed from me. But I was using her, and my guilt was another incarnation of loneliness. I was a dying, middle-aged man taking a last communion. But in the instant of climax, when I felt transformed into the neon light all around me, wan and pulsing, straining for my ending, for it all to be done, I heard the old man I had killed whispering his last word.

And I opened my eyes and raised my head and saw my mother, ashes floating like dust, filling this room like a furnace with the red light of death and distance.

I closed my eyes tightly and saw a death's head in the red-limned darkness.

CHAPTER SIX
BOGEY-MAN

We parted company with Bob early the next morning. Bob looked burned out, yet he offered to join us, if we would wait for him to conclude his deal. I thanked him, and then he offered to fly in and pick us up. "Sure," I said, not believing that I would ever see him again; and we lost each other in the streets.

The vendors had been out for hours, and as it was a Saturday, there were so many of them that Genaro and I had to watch where we stepped, lest we walk upon the vari-colored blankets displaying goods and, perhaps, break something. We passed tanned Italian tourists wearing leisure suits, Americans wearing bush jackets and baggy pants, and Japanese as well as native Brazilian tourists, all of whom had come to the wild and dangerous jungle to vacation and shop. We passed stands of vegetables and fruits where Indian vendors shouted and haggled with prospective buyers. We passed people selling crocodile skulls, shells, snake skins, musical instruments, herbs and potions, and I almost gagged as we went through a fish-market where seventy pound *tambaquis* catfish lay on long slippery stands alongside eel and turtle and piranha and fish that had probably never been catalogued—ugly, ancient-looking, spiny creatures that looked reptilian. Young boys were running around and loud music seemed to be blasting out of every doorway.

I followed Genaro to the concrete wharfs where we might find a boat. There was a haze on the river, although it was late morning, and the *barcos*—the small boats and barges, which were in various states of disrepair—were packed into the quays, as if they were but a floating extension of shantytown. A speedboat passed slowly by with two uniformed men watching the shore: agency police patrolling the river for smugglers and poachers. I looked around at the nearby *barcos*: many of them were barges with a motor; some had two or three decks, all with the ubiquitous, colorful hammocks, upon which people were lying down and drinking and listening to portable radios. Even here music was a background. The sounds of canned easy-listening music mingled with samba, rock, and jazz-fusion. A beautiful *mameluco* woman breastfeeding a baby watched us from the deck of a small motor, which was covered with stacked boxes and grayish-white squares of sorva, a gum often used for calking and the basic stuff of *chicle*. A few fishing boats were anchored, but most were up river and long gone. In fact, although young boys were all about, shouting and catcalling each other as they packed and unpacked cases of soda, beer, supplies, and food from a large boat—this a passenger ship, with a high smokestack, several decks decorated with brass fittings and filigree, that plied the water between here and Santarem—there were few men in the area. There were many women working here, though: cooking, putting out wash, working on the boats, selling and trading fish and palm nuts and jute for sugar and salt and kerosene.

Genaro talked to a short, stocky man of about forty, who had no upper front teeth and was quite drunk. His missing teeth made his lower jaw appear to jut out. He looked like a *brancinho*, for his frizzy gray-flecked hair was red, his skin was ruddy and freckled, but his features were Negroid. He stood on the flat deck of a thirty foot motor, which had a cabin consisting of kitchen and toilet in the back and a wheelhouse in the front; the deck was covered with a torn canvass roof that ballooned in the wind and made cracking and whipping sounds. Genaro's friend had left months ago for Santarem and had never returned, the man told us. "He found a girl," he said, making a quick obscene gesture with both of his oddly delicate yet calloused hands, "and he left his wife and children alone." Then he spat and shook his head.

"Do you know of a boat we can rent?" I asked, and Genaro gave me a quick but angry glance, for my impatience might queer the deal and certainly cost us more money. But I *was* impatient. There was something about being here at the edge of the city, watching the water, which made me slightly dizzy, as if the land were undulating, and I felt trapped and claustrophobic. I wanted to get away from the smell of chemicals and fish and people; I wanted to ply the dark water of the Amazon. I wanted this last journey...this last chase, if, indeed, that was what it was. And if these strange dreams of Onca's, Genaro's, and my own were true, I wanted to be justice for Mengele.

Then I could rest in peace.

The man looked at Genaro and shook his head. "*Onde vai?*" he asked.

"*Wakatauteri,*" Genaro said, and he nodded toward the river.

The man shook his head again. "*Perigoso.*" Then after a pause, he said, "*Quanto custa?*"

Genaro looked at me and said, "1500 cruzeiros."

The sailor laughed and lit a flattened cigarette; I had seen Turkish cigarettes rolled that way. "7,500," he said. They argued. Genaro told him that we wanted to rent the boat, but didn't want him as captain. The sailor threw down his cigarette and started walking toward the cabin. "What do you want to do?" Genaro asked me.

"5,000," I said. "*Estou com pressa.*"

"*Americano,*" he said. He looked at Genaro scornfully; Genaro did not meet his eyes. "6,000," the sailor said. I nodded, and the deal was done, although for what I was paying he could buy a new boat.

An hour later we were on the river, chugging out of the harbor. The engine skipped and choked, and Genaro had to adjust the carburetor while I took the wheel. We were in Amazon waters, which were brown and muddy, the color of light chocolate; but the Rio

Negro flowed beside us, and its surface was like a black mirror. And like oil and water poured into the same trough, the rivers remained separate because of their different temperatures and speeds. We passed warehouses, factories, oil refineries, sawmills, and as we put distance between ourselves and the city, we passed farms and the occasional white stucco house with red tiled roof, which reminded me of home. There were plenty of fishing boats and barges on the river; some families had tied two, three, and in some cases, four boats together, and they floated down the river like the ragtag retinue of an ancient king. We waved at the passers-by, who were lying in colored cotton hammocks; or drinking *caipirinhas*, concoctions made with rum, sugar, and lemon; or playing dominoes, which wouldn't blow away in a stiff wind, like cards. I felt the distance from everything familiar as we went into deeper country. We passed isolated cottages with penned cattle and neatly planted trees and then crossed over to the Rio Negro side, for we were going to take a branch of the Negro, the Rio Branco, north. The shore consisted of a green swatch of vegetation and trees of different hues of green and different heights. We motored toward the Branco and as we went farther into the rain-forest, it became warmer with every mile, and the humidity was so high that my shirt clung to my skin like a transparent wrap. There was nothing to do but stay in one place and try not to move around too much. We kept as close as we dared to the clay river bank, slowly passing by and sometimes under cool, shady canopies of tree branches, roots, and vines. The trees beyond were so closely packed as to cut out the light, a wall of leaf and bole that seemed to rise into the cloudless eggshell blue heavens.

We passed a few Indians paddling dugouts; the canoes were made out of hollowed-out itauba wood, which was black and hard as stone. By dusk we met a river merchant, a *cabloclo* with his wife and three daughters, who sold us some gasoline; and then we were alone on the river, which became dark, the color of dried blood, for as the sun set, the sky turned from blue to orange to deep crimson. The color seemed to be visible as a fine mist in the air; it was as if we were passing into a different atmosphere, and ahead of us and far to the left, almost in the center of the river, we saw river dolphins playing, breaking the surface. They came closer to us, as if looking for company, and swam and jumped and splashed and made snorting noises. Then, almost impossibly fast, they left, disappearing into the glassy water.

Genaro smiled and said, "*Botos*. Black ones. You can tell by the way they stick their heads above the water; the pink boto they come to the surface differently. You see their back first. The pink ones, they are almost gone, but where we're going, they may still live because it's so far away from the fishermen. After a pause he said, "The black ones are almost gone, too." He stuffed a loose wad of chewing tobacco into the side of his mouth, chewed for a bit, making sucking noises, and then spat into the dark water. The river seemed to change Genaro, animate him somehow, as if being close to its teeming life gave him life also. The deadness that sometimes clung to him had disappeared; his movements were less cautious and studied, and he was talking, almost to himself, as if for the joy of hearing his voice once again. If I had not known him at the facenda, I would take him to be gregarious, a man who enjoys company, but one who is not altogether giving, one who has been hurt and defeated... one whose defenses are like jaws that snap shut at the merest intimation of violation.

Night came almost at once, and I imagined I could see after-images of the red sunset on the surface of the river. A full moon bathed river and jungle in a wan, pearly light. We were near the Rio Alatau, which was a tributary of the Branco, and there we anchored. We could hear the jungle all around us, the constant sawing and chirruping of insects and frogs and every so often the heart-stopping cries of howler monkeys. I felt as if we were a thousand miles from any civilization, as if the world I had just left was an ancient dream, a fogged memory. We tucked down the canvass as best we could to keep out mosquitoes—they did not seem to be out in force here, which was also one of our reasons for staying here the night. I had doused myself several times during the day with insect repellant, and I did so again, just to be safe. Genaro made dinner, a delicious catfish called *jandia*, which he had caught earlier. He fried it and surrounded our plates with slices of fruit, but he warned me not to bite into the husk of the cashwe fruit, for "it would burn like fire." But I couldn't finish my meal, as good as it was, for my stomach began aching; and I spent an hour aft. The pain was followed by waves of nausea, and when I finally felt strong enough to return, I was chilled and sweating. I was going to take a pill for pain, but Genaro had made a bowl of Onca's manioc gruel and said, "Eat a little if you can. "Onca mixed up this for you; better than the pills." I forced down a little, although it gagged me, yet within a few minutes I felt relief. "I'm sorry, but no ice cream here," Genaro said. I smiled and lay down in my hammock; I could still feel pain, but it seemed isolated, controlled.

"Onca's a fine woman," I said rather lamely, but I wanted to talk about her with Genaro, pull him a bit about her.

Genaro nodded and said, "She likes you, or she wouldn't have stayed with you for so long. She had an offer to go to Belém to work for a factory owner. You see, she worked for very rich people before. She never told you that, no? But she thinks of you as if...as if you need to be *preocupar-se com*, how do you say, ah, mothered. That's what. Like you're the child, even though you're a man and have killed other men."

I looked sharply up at him.

"Onca told me this from her dream, but I would know anyway."

"And how's that," I asked, edgy.

"The way you are. I can see it sometimes, just as you can see me. What do you see from me?"

He had caught me off-guard. But, yes, I did see something. There was a connection between us. I had felt it when we had talked in my dining room. I sensed his psychic heaviness then, his burden, which was somehow like my own. And I felt that connection now once again, although the burden seemed lighter; perhaps because we felt free. An illusion, most likely, but I sensed it nevertheless.

"Well?" he asked in earnest. It certainly seemed that the river had dissolved some of his sullenness. "I see us both carrying something terrible with us," I said, suddenly embarrassed. "As if we share this...thing in common. A darkness, perhaps."

Genaro nodded, seemingly satisfied. "You see," he said. "You can see. But where we're going, that is where I found the darkness, the burden."

"What do you mean?" I asked.

He didn't answer that; he just leaned back against the bulkhead and looked up at the stars, which were as bright and cold-looking as bits of ice reflecting some strong, focused light. He was silent.

"Why are you going back then?" I asked, persisting.

After a long pause he said, "To take back the burden." Then he moved away from me and drank his rum from the bottle by himself. Suddenly I had a sense of déja vu, and I realized that right now, I was living the dream I had had of being on the river. The smells and sounds of the river and jungle were exactly right. They disoriented me, for in that instant of realization I couldn't discern whether I was dreaming or awake.

And as I lay in my damp hammock, I remembered my other recurring dreams, I remembered my brother David being electrocuted by Mengele in a house that was by appearances my own, and I broke into cold sweat. I could *feel* Mengele's presence here, suffocating me, and I shivered, once again a child in the camp. Yet I could not hate him then, for I was too frightened, anxious, as if he were my father, as everything here—the insects, the lapping water, the splashing fish and screeing monkeys—were all simply manifestation of Mengele. As if I were but a manifestation of Uncle Pepe, of Mengele, the jungle itself.

Suddenly a great crashing noise startled me. At first I thought some animal was smashing through brush. That noise was followed by an almost human wail that was so unearthly that I found myself standing on the deck, the sweat sending chills down my spine. I had never heard a sound like it, and I wanted to leave this place immediately.

Genaro was up and walking forward to the wheelhouse. He started the motor, and we glided out to the center of the river, which reflected the stars; it seemed we were drifting in space among them.

"What was that noise?" I asked.

"*Curupira*," he said matter-of-factly. "Bogey-man. That's his noise. Not usual to hear his noise, and we're so early on the river. But now we leave everything behind here. From now on this is a place for bugs and monsters. You will see the monsters, or see some of them already. You think this is crazy?" Genaro asked.

I shrugged, trying to get that wailing noise out of my mind. I thought back to when I had first heard the howler monkeys, how their shrieks had jolted me, but this sound was different. I couldn't imagine it coming from anything known to science. It did have a beauty, though, as did the inhuman lowing of white whales. Yet, somehow, this sound was...sinister.

"The *curupira* is dreams, that's all," Genaro continued. When you hear it you dream of dying. It helps you die, but it cannot kill you. Not like the *cobra grande*, which I myself once saw. Now that is a real thing in the world. It is like a dragon and over a hundred feet long. Its eyes are *azulado*, like fireflies blinking. And it kills those on the river. I've seen it turn over boats and make food for the piranha. And I've also seen the *Mapinguari*, the monster with one eye that lives in the jungle. I saw him gore a man. When I breathed the doctor's red dust, I saw these things, too. I saw snakes crawling through the air and disappear like smoke. I saw a man see these things and die and come to life again."

"What about the doctor's red dust?" I asked, wondering if Genaro was a little crazy, or perhaps it was just the normal run of superstition one acquires in this part of the world. Certainly Genaro had no education; like Onca, he couldn't read or write, except to make a squiggle that signified his name.

Most likely he had seen some of his monsters on hallucinogens.

But this was the first time he had mentioned the

doctor on his own, and so I tried to get him to continue.

"If we get to where we're going, maybe you'll see," Genaro said. "Me, I think the doctor made these monsters to keep Indians away. Maybe he changed his mind later and couldn't kill them. Who knows but *Deus* and the doctor?"

"Tell me what you remember about the doctor?" I asked.

Genaro had his back turned to me.

"Genaro?"

"I remember what I tell you. The rest I cannot remember."

Or will not, I thought.

Genaro took a sip from his bottle of *cachaça* as he piloted the boat up the dead-quiet river. The water was like black glass, and the silence was as palpable as the darkness.

* * * * * * *

I slept most of the night to the constant throbbing of the engine and the breaking of water against the hull. I came awake sharply a few times, twice screaming, but I couldn't remember what, if anything I had dreamed, and feeling uneasy and anxious, I fell back to sleep, to finally wake up well after dawn. Although we had put up the canvass to keep out the bugs, they had easily gotten inside. I brushed six or seven transparent pium flies from my face and arms. Looking closely, I could see the abdomen's of the creatures filled with blood, my blood. The bites itched, and I was covered with tiny welts. I got up and pulled down the canvass.

"I think sometimes the canvass makes them worse," Genaro said, looking back at me from the wheel. It's like we built a house for them to live in. You should put alcohol on yourself, Meester."

"I have some insect repellent," I said.

"Alcohol works much better. Stop the itch then drink some. Then you can use the other stuff."

I noticed that the cloud of insects wasn't swirling around him. Perhaps it was something about his metabolism or sweat that kept them away. But they were devouring me.

"We'll be out of it soon, Genaro said. "These bugs, they don't like to travel too far."

He was right, and I did as he said. Indeed, the alcohol eased the itching and burning, but the sores from my pemphigus which had been stung were especially painful. The day passed uneventfully. Genaro kept to the east side of the Branco for shade and the west shore later in the afternoon. I kept to the hammock, for I was trying to conserve my strength, what I had left. I ate Onca's gruel and while I perspired in the choking heat and humidity, my insides felt cool and anesthetized. I wasn't anxious, or frightened. Perhaps it was the river; perhaps I had absorbed its calm, its rhythm. Genaro seemed in his element here, and to watch him, one could believe he was happy, for the time being at least. He would turn to me every few minutes and nod or curl his upper lip, which for him was the equivalent of a smile. We didn't talk much after last night, except some small talk, which petered out, for it sounded so inane against the backdrop of river and perfectly clear sky and mud banks and dense forest, a wall I could not imagine penetrating. We passed a few black caymans, ugly alligators baking in the sun, and turtles, whose eggs were an illegal native staple, for they were becoming an endangered species. But here in the wilds, life was in profusion. Pink macaws shouted, flycatchers crashed through shrubs as we passed, and all manner of bird cawed and screed and made creaking unbird-like sounds: jaos and hoatzins and Orinoco geese. Kingfishers flew close to the surface of the water, and I caught a glimpse of a huge black snake slithering between two rocks. The snake had to be fifteen feet long. It was easy to imagine how one could exaggerate size here...to imagine a great black snake that was a hundred feet long, that swam just below the surface of the river until it sensed a barco to capsize in its waters. And I even glimpsed a jaguar, or thought I did, and I remembered its caged cousin near the entrance to my hotel.

As the day wore on, my thoughts seemed to move back to memory, and I thought of my ex-wife Adriana. The river seemed to open me up, for I felt a sense of loss over her, as if it were only days rather than years since she left me. She had loved me more that I could love her, for I was obsessed with my work, with Mossad, as if by finding Mengele, I could rework my life again from the beginning. And indeed that's what I had promised her. I would change. I would be ready for a family and a permanent home. Now, twenty years too late, I ached for her, for the pretty little kitchen she had made, for the way she stared at me when she thought I wasn't looking, for the security and love she had tried to give me. And I remember how I had felt when she left. Lonely, a bit, but relieved. I had become like iron *after* I survived. I had survived Mengele and died. And the river reminded me. It seemed to sing with voices I only now remembered, and on this sun-scorching day, as we motored through primeval land, I wanted to close my eyes and be done with myself. It was no longer guilt, but a profound sense of loss, a loss of everyone I had loved, a loss, finally, of self.

We passed a hut in the center of a clearing beyond the mud flats of the river. It's sides were mud and wattle, and it looked like a beehive that was secured to the ground by a huge wishbone, which was in actuality a tree cut down from the forest beyond. Green parrots and pink and turquoise macaws perched on the limbs straddling the hut and screamed at each other. The roof was covered with palm leaves. Food and waste littered the ground around the hut. A primitive pier reached over the water like an unfinished bridge; a canoe bobbed up and down in the water beside it, and a man stood at the pier's edge. He watched us and waved. Although he wore only torn, baggy trousers belted with twine, and seemed to be in good physical shape, I could not even begin to guess his age. His face was so disfigured that he looked like a creature that had escaped from one of Goya's etching plates into the bright sunlight. His nose and the upper part of his mouth had been eaten away, turning him into a monster that looked like he was always screaming silently, or perhaps luridly laughing. The horrifying effect was heightened by the few misshapen teeth that remained in his lower jaw. He must have contracted leishmaniasis, a parasitic disease that was not uncommon in this part of the world. But I had never seen the disease progress this far. I couldn't help but think, as I watched him standing beside his small boat, that this was the River Lethe rather than a tributary of the Amazon, and this twilight creature waving to us was Charon, hailing us down.

I found myself waving back.

"It's bad luck to look at him," Genaro said.

"What do you mean?" I asked.

"He's like the bogey-man. He's a dream thing. I know him. I've seen him before."

Then we rounded a curve in the river and the grotesque and his hut and pier and boat were gone, as if they had been heat ghosts on a highway, and for an instant I believed that if we turned around and went back, we would not find anything but mud-flats and river and forest. But it was not the place that was magical or irreal—not Brazil, not the river, not the jungle; it was my impending death, my closeness to it, that was turning me into a *bruxa*, a sorcerer, a lucid dreamer. I drew a raw and complicated strength from it; and it connected me like an umbilicus to my boyhood, to the camps, to Mengele. For there I had survived as a dreamer, swimming between dream and reality as if they were flowing side by side like the Negro and Amazon. I was a child demon, a denizen of my waking nightmares, just as was Mengele, who created them. He had been pulled into his own dark and evil magicks, and it gave him the blind, monomaniacal strength to tower above rules and morality, to become as cruel as Heinrich Hoffman's *Struwwelpeter* storybook characters, which we had both grown up with. Good and evil were simply opposed manifestations of power: the interjection of dreams into the world.

I watched a group of large yellow butterflies flitter across the water before us and then swoop up into the air like dust devils being carried by the wind. And Genaro was right, for I suddenly and with a shock remembered last night's dreams that had been working themselves out of me like a psychic peristalsis all morning. It was one dream, recurring, Onca's dream. I was in this boat, just as I am. In fact everything was exactly as it is: the suffocating humidity, the smell of Carter Insect Repellant and alcohol, the reflections of light on the water, the mudbanks and grotesquely shaped roots and vines that hung into the water like the limbs of some infinitely long slithering creature.

But I had the same face as the man on the shore.

I had waved to myself.

Death was turning me into the man on the shore, baking my bones brown; it would soon dissolve my flesh, a cosmic leishmaniasis.

CHAPTER SEVEN
THE DREAM FOREST

We traveled up the Branco to the Catrimani River, which went north and then west until we were in Wakatauteri country, which was near the eastern border of Venezuela. We stayed the night on the river and put to shore at dawn. Genaro scattered amulets over the deck: stones and herbs and a worn skull, undeniably human; I was surprised he would have been carrying such a thing, but I made no mention of it.

"We have to leave the boat in the open here, nothing else to do," Genaro said. "We could try to cover it, but no use. People, they know we're coming. I see them in the bush before."

"You never mentioned it to me," I said.

"Not necessary to say anything. But Aitaí people, they're around."

"Will we see them?" I asked, as we divided up our packs. Genaro took the heaviest, but I wanted to carry my weight too.

"There's a mission here, and many Yanomano there," Genaro said. Yanomano are Aitaí, too. But nobody's supposed to go there unless you have government papers. To make sure you don't mess up the Indian culture." He raised his lip after he said that, obviously pleased with himself. "They're teaching Indians how to get along with white people, teaching them how to use money, but there it's the white people who live in cages to keep out the Indians. It's stupid, but they're afraid, the government's afraid, that those pure Indians will get corrupted and get like me. Although I'm not pure, anyway. But I was at that place once, and unless we're in some big trouble I wouldn't go back. Who knows, they may all be dead by now anyway. Maybe killed. Or disease. Or maybe all the Indians leave their *maloccas* and go back to the trees, make their own villages again. That probably wouldn't happen."

I followed him through the bush and then we were making our way through the forest. It was dim and cooler here than on the river; the weather suddenly changed. It was raining, pouring, but very little reached us under the hundred foot high canopy of trees. The smell of decaying leaves and logs and dampness pervaded everything. The smell of the soil was dampness itself, and then in minutes the temperature cooled down some twenty degrees. It was tough going for the first few hours; I had to stop every half-hour or so, but the pills numbed my pain and Genaro had given me a root to chew on, which made me feel stronger and eased my queasiness. Perhaps it had an effect similar to cocaine. But then we found a trail, which was cleared, although I wouldn't have recognized it if I had been alone. "This goes to the mission," he said, and we traveled that for a ways and then detoured back into 'uninhabited' country. There was a sameness to the forest: the great boles of trees, the roots and leaves on the forest floor, a few blades of heliconia, a few flowers, but this was lowland forest, all green and brown, uniform, for the bursting of colors, the flowers and wildly hued birds were all above us, in the canopy, out of our reach. It was also quiet, only the crush of leaves and branches and pine-cones underfoot, the occasional unnerving scream of the pia, the hissing of insects, the thrumming of *jacamins*, those were the only sounds. The silence of the place made it difficult to talk; it was like a weight that had to be pressed against with words, and I was concentrating on putting one foot before the other, on getting through for the next few minutes. But I had to call to Genaro every few minutes or so because he naturally tended to walk fast, especially when we reached savannah, which seemed like an ocean of fifteen-foot high grass. My first sensation was of agoraphobia, after being in the forest, which was somehow like walking through thousands upon thousands of rooms. My mind had used the trees as imaginary demarcations and filled in the cognitive spaces.

It rained, sheets of water, for over an hour; the wind was strong and its gusts felt somehow jagged rather than sweeping. The savannah bowed to the storm, making the windpaths visible, boiling the stalks like a storm on the river. Thunderheads loomed above, gray with a misting of pink from the sun, and they moved quickly, leaving me with the impression that they could have been parted by God's hands. Then the sky became completely clear, and the humidity returned like air blown through an exhaust pipe. The sky, suffused with pink, gave way to a pellucid clear blue; and the savannah glistened as if covered with dew. It was like walking through a painting of the clarity and intensity of a Vermeer. The hugeness of sky, the rolling grass and jungle climbing into hills seemed to stop time, made me feel as if I were suspended in perfection, that this was the form from which the rest of the world had been, imperfectly, made.

We followed a winding path made by ants, which looked like a white chalk-line that had been dropped by some impossible craftsman, and Genaro navigated it as easily as if he were steering the *barco* we had rented. He would put one foot exactly in front of the other, which gave him extraordinary speed and balance; the same reason why American Indians do so well walking on high girders. It was an entirely different way of walking. As I couldn't keep up with him, he had to slow his pace until I could see it was plainly agonizing for him. He had found a few moments of freedom here, and, once again, I was restricting him. But even walking slowly, I had a tendency to drift off the ant-path and trip and smash into hidden vines, roots, and branches.

"You must be careful of snakes here, Meester," Genaro said. "Not so many here that can hurt you, but you walk like a drunk man off the path and step on one of them and they'll bite you good." I had once stepped on a fer de lance at my fazenda; luckily I had been wearing high leather boots, or I would have been dead. It had drooled a scummy yellow venom all over my boot. In the savannah, I might encounter *cascavel*, or rattler, and maybe *cobras-corais*, which can be pulled away from the skin before it expands its mouth, if the potential victim is fast enough. I had medicine for snakebite, including antihistamine for shock; but even under the best of circumstances, the chances of surviving were only about fifty percent.

But as we neared the forest, he slowed his pace, at times stopping entirely and cocking his head, as if listening for something. I asked him what was wrong, but he only said, "Dreams. Can't you feel them?"

"What do you mean?" I asked as I looked at the forest looming beyond the savannah; it seemed endless. Above the forest, layers of cloud had gathered like smoke. Although I had always felt good being near primal land such as this, I now felt something ominous; it was as if with every step we took toward the jungle ahead, we were getting nearer to darkness and heaviness.

I had felt that before.

In the camps.

"You feel them or you don't," Genaro said. It was as if these dreams he was feeling were closing him up once again, for his manner, his posture, even his face took on the sullenness I had known at the fazenda. Whatever he was feeling, or fighting, had clouded him;

and I felt the old, traditional barriers between us, the silence of companionship suddenly and irrevocably replaced by the silence of isolation.

Genaro was in a shell, and I knew as we entered the darkness of the forest that we were near our destination. This forest was identical to every other I had been in over the years, with one exception: this one didn't seem quite real. It smelled like earth and leaf and compost; macaws crashed through brush above and screeched like metal penetrating metal; but somehow it all felt wrong. Dreamlike, that was it. Everything was in place; everything was perfect, except for one minor and yet impossible thing. What that was I didn't know...yet.

So yes I felt the dreams, I supposed. But I couldn't tell Genaro I understood; he was too locked into himself. He was the old hollow-eyed, tight-faced Genaro, and worse. We were getting closer to the source of his burden. I could feel that, and I wanted to comfort him. But it was no use. And I knew that although Genaro wouldn't have come this far on his own, that he was here for me out of a sense of *direito*, of duty and honor, he was here now for himself. Perhaps Onca's scream that night was for Genaro, for the death he was carrying. We both carried it, only mine was manifest on my skin and in my organs.

We walked through the forest until dark, with frequent stops, and then made camp near a stream that gurgled and fell over black rocks, a small white waterfall of foam and spray. White noise. We set up our tent, built a fire, and Genaro and I ate some of our canned rations. The darkness seemed absolute, bringing with it the constant chittering of insects and the skreeing of bats overhead. I couldn't see the sky, as the canopy of trees effectively blocked it out, and the shadows cast by the fire before me gave the nearby trees a quality of constant motion. I imagined that the monsters Genaro had talked about were lurking all around us, and I would jump when I heard a branch or leaves being crunched underfoot. And I could see the red reflections of fire in the eyes of forest creatures watching us. I took a pill for pain and chewed on the bark Genaro had given me to quell the nausea.

"Genaro, do you have any idea where we really are?"

Genaro didn't look up at me, but stirred the fire with a charred stick.

"Well?" I asked.

"Aitaí country here," Genaro said, after a time. "Aitaí people want to see you, give you dreams, see what you do with them. Best to be asleep when they do that or makes you crazy like drugs. So best we go to sleep," and with that he crawled inside the tent. End of conversation.

But I wasn't ready to sleep yet. I looked around and listened to the stream. The fire was low, so I broke a few branches and tossed them into the weak flames. Maybe someone was out there, for I felt as if I was being stared at. I went to the edge of the firelight, looking about. Then, exhausted, I crawled into the tent. I lay on the damp ground in my sleeping bag and listened to the mosquitoes buzzing and vibrating against the tent canvass. I could smell my sweat and Genaro's, sweet and fetid; mine was mixed with the almost gasoline odor of insect repellant. I chewed on the medicine Genaro gave me and waited for sleep and dreams.

I stared wide-eyed into darkness.

I slept fitfully and was awakened once by Genaro sobbing and moaning and talking and thrashing beside me. Perhaps the Aitaí were giving him dreams, as he said they would.

We both woke up just before dawn.

"I heard you moaning and talking in your sleep," I told Genaro.

He just grunted, obviously not willing to discuss his dreams, nor curious about what he might have said; although I couldn't have told him anything, anyway, as I could only make out slurred words and moans. After we crawled out of the tent he asked, "Did you have dreams, Meester?"

I had not dreamed at all, at least not that I could remember, and that's what I told him.

"If you dreamed, you would remember Aitaí."

"What do you remember?" I asked.

"Aitaí are here, you'll see," Genaro said. "But you must have had dreams."

"Not that I can remember."

"Then maybe *this* is your dream," Genaro said.

I looked up at him, expecting his raised lip grin. But his face was as vacant as a somnambulist.

* * * * * * *

We broke camp after dawn, as a dusky light filtered through the trees, turning everything sallow, as if a cinematographer were using yellow lenses for strange effect. I hoisted my pack—which was much lighter than Genaro's—to my shoulders, and seven Indian men stepped out of the forest into our clearing. They appeared out of the bush without a sound, as if they were spirits. Their faces were heavily painted and tattooed, their oiled black hair was cut straight across the forehead; some of the men wore shirts or pants, others wore penis sheaths, balsa earplugs, long fans of palm splinters stuck into lips, and one wore a lip disk, which gave him a terrifying appearance, reminding me of the man with the rotted face I had seen on the river. They all carried shotguns, which they held in a sort of port arms position. Suddenly they started shouting at us and making menacing faces. I reached for my pistol reactively, but Genaro grabbed my hand and said, "They're making greeting. White people are backwards from Aitaí. Aitaí shake their heads when they mean yes. This is showing a bad face now so it won't be for real."

The Aitaí cracked their rifles, and, with the stock swiveled down, they made resounding noises by blaring through the barrels. Birds screeched above, as if in response.

And then another Indian stepped into the clearing. The others moved out of his way, showing him defer-ence...either out of fear or respect. He wore no face or body paint to frighten his enemies; he didn't need to, for half of his face and body was like that of a young man's while the other side was withered, blotched, and wrinkled. Even his hair, which was black on one side, was a yellowish white on the other; perhaps he had dyed it, but he could not have faked the rest. The wrinkles and flaccid flesh of old age contrasted with the muscle tone and energy of youth; it was as if the younger side was bearing the weight of the older. Indeed, he favored the 'young' side of his body. I could not imagine what disease could have such an effect, and I felt as if I were looking at some kind of mythical demiurge.

But the demiurge was staring back at me so intently that I had to look away.

"What the hell happened to *him*?" I whispered to Genaro, unnerved.

The other Indians were watching us silently, as if waiting for us to make the first move.

"He's a *claro sonhador*," Genaro said.

"What?"

"Like a dreamer. Only he lives his dream to its end."

Then Genaro turned to him, spoke a few words, and then exchanged greetings with the other Indians, one by one. He presented me to all of them, except the *sonhador*; and the tension seemed to ease a bit, although the Indians stood in place as if they were in formation.

We exchanged gifts, as was customary.

We gave them each a cigarette lighter, a plastic watch, a few nails and needles, and a colored comb. We would save the shorts and dresses, hammock, flashlights, and tape recorder for the chief, should we meet him.

They didn't give anything to Genaro, but the dreamer came over to me and sat down on his haunches. I watched him take two arrows out of his quiver, which he had laid beside him, and begin rubbing the points together over a large, veined banana leaf. A small pile of rust-colored powder began to form on the leaf. The other men were now standing around us, as if acting as protection in case a gust of wind were to scatter the powder.

"What's all this?" I asked Genaro, but he just shook his head and nodded in the direction of the dreamer who was rubbing the points together. He pressed against my shoulder, which meant that I should squat down on the ground. I relieved myself of my pack and sat down before the dreamer.

"He's making you a gift," Genaro said as he squatted beside me. "*Um outro mundo.* He's giving you another world. Dreams you can remember."

"What is that stuff," I asked nervously.

"They call it *washaharua.* When they shoot a bird or an animal with it, it makes the animal relax and fall down."

It must contain something like tryptamine, I thought. I'd heard of that, but never of using the stuff as a hallucinogen. "I'm not taking anything," I said.

"Not a good idea to refuse."

"Why?"

"They would kill both of us," Genaro said matter-of-factly.

"What about you?" I asked. "Are you going to participate in whatever they've cooked up?"

"The gift is for you, Meester. I had the gifts of dreams last night. You did not, that's what you said."

The dreamer expertly cut the pile in half with his fingernail, which was over an inch long, and he pushed each pile to opposite sides of the leaf. Then he inhaled the stuff into each nostril and offered the leaf and the remaining pile of the drug to me. I hesitated, but I had no choice.

I inhaled the powder.

Once I did so the group broke up. The dreamer walked to the other side of the clearing, sat down against a tree, and watched me.

I sat where I was. My nostrils burned, and I felt as if my sinuses were contracting. I fought nausea, which stopped after a few minutes, and waited for the drug to take effect. The dreamer was still staring at me, and I noticed that his eyes had taken on a brilliant cast; unlike the other men, his eyes glittered with a feral intensity, like the eyes of animals reflected by a fire at night. And then his head lolled, and he fell asleep, closing off the gem-like fire burning inside his head, for at that moment I was certain that his eyes were like openings or grates in a furnace. I looked around. No one was moving. I was inside time, although I heard a humming inside my head, a beautiful minor melody, and then realized that I was hearing myself moaning. I felt weightless, as if I could leave the pain and constraints of my body, which I did. I found myself looking down at my body, which seemed to be decomposing as I watched. Everything around me looked preternaturally brilliant; every leaf and root and tree and creature exuded its own separate hue; together, everything and everyone in the forest radiated brilliant white light. Each one of us, every creature and tree and insect were streams of refracted light.

And I walked away from myself...walked toward the dreamer, who was waiting for me. We walked out of the clearing through the forest, which was blazing in its component hues, as if my eyes were prisms separating the frozen light.

"You think you did not dream last night," the dreamer said.

"How do you know English?" I asked, and then realized that his mouth hadn't moved. This was a dream. But was I dreaming when I first saw him? Was *he* a dream?

I was drugged, stoned.

Nothing to do but go with it.

"What do you think you dreamed?" the dreamer asked.

"I don't know," I answered. "I can't remember dreaming anything."

"This is what you dreamed."

"What?"

"What you're doing now," he said. "We saw your dream. Only you did not see it."

"I don't know what you're talking about. Where are we going?"

The dreamer made a sound like "hnrung, hnrung," which I presumed was laughter. "It's *your* dream. We gave it to you to see what happens."

"Is that why you look the way you do?" I asked him. "Because it's my dream."

He made the "hnrung, hnrung" sound again and said, "No, I look the way I do because of *my* dream. You give yourself too much importance, Meester. Now why are you in this place?"

"I'm looking for someone," I said. The dreamer had found a narrow trail, which was probably the way to his village. The trees, grass, and leaves still seemed frozen, and perfect; and although I walked over mulch and leaf, it was more like I was passing over, for this was a place I could not really enter. I was here, yet somehow contiguous to everything, not a part of anything.

"Who?"

"A man," I said. "His name is Mengele."

"And for what do you want him for."

"To kill him." I suddenly felt a rush of anger, which was like syrup freezing inside me. The drug, I said to myself, yet I genuinely couldn't wake up, couldn't find myself other than here in this frozen forest with the dreamer who had dreamed himself into an old man...or into a young man.

"That's all?" he asked.

"To free myself," I said.

"And you care for nothing else but his death?"

"No."

"Perhaps to live?"

"Perhaps...."

"Then go there."

"Where?" I asked.

The dreamer was favoring his young side and seemed to be using his old side merely for balance. He pointed toward the trail we had been walking on, which widened ahead. I turned away from him and began to walk.

That's when I felt the thud of a blunt object across the back of my head.

Perhaps it was the drug.

I saw radiant whiteness

Which faded into blinding pain.

CHAPTER EIGHT
MIRRORS OF THE PAST

I awakened in a four-poster bed curtained with white clouds of mosquito netting. Beside me was a high window that overlooked a large English-style garden. My first impression of the hedges and shrubs outside was that they were part of some kind of circular maze. It was near dusk. The room was filled with a gray, western light, and the netting added even more to the effect of twilight softness. But I felt as if the light had mass and was pressing against me. I could feel the weight of the room as if it were a great sadness, my own grief given space to expand. I could smell it, see it, and hear it....

I heard the creaking of floorboards and saw a phantom shape enter the room, and suddenly the curtains were pulled away and I was looking up wide-eyed at the Indian who had given me the drug and entered my hallucinatory dream. He was wearing a white shirt closed at the neck and khaki pants, perfectly cut. As he stood over me, offering me a robe, I could see that, indeed, half of his face was that of an old man and the other half was that of a young man. His appearance had not been a dream. I also noticed a black mole on the young side of his face, just under his right eye. But the brilliant luster of his eyes had dimmed. I could no longer peer into the furnace of his mind through a dream induced by his rust-colored drug, only gaze at what were now dead embers, black and flecked with gold, as if perhaps they could catch fire again.

I sat up and took the robe, and he said, "The *Doutor* is waiting for you. I will help you dress and take you to him."

"Who is this...*Doutor*?" I asked, but he just looked at me uncomprehending, as if I had asked the unaskable. I asked him where I was and how I had gotten here, but he just shook his head and ordered me to wash in the adjoining bathroom. "And where is my friend Genaro?" I asked.

He said, "Your friend is very fine, but you find out everything from the *Doutor*," and he helped, or rather forced me to the bathroom. I was weak and woozy, most likely still under the effect of the drug, and he was surprisingly strong; I could not pull away from him, nor could I take him off balance. "Please, do not fight me, Meester," he said. "I have seen you in your dream. You wanted to be in this place. I saw that."

I mumbled something back to him, but a wave of nausea passed over me. I remembered dreaming, hallucinating, but I could only remember bits and pieces of what I had dreamed, impressions that had the same 'feel' as childhood memories which had been embroidered by the years into almost surrealistic, numinal images. I remember the Indian, the dreamer, a nightmarish Janus pointing out the way to this place, standing in a forest that seemed frozen, crystalline, his arm raised toward some destination outside of the dream.

He left me alone in the tiled bathroom and closed the door with a click. Most likely locked it, I thought.

I leaned on the sink and looked into the mirror. I smelled of illness, of unhealthy sweat. My stomach felt numb; I surmised that to be one of the effects of the drug, for I wasn't in pain, yet I could think clearly, or so it seemed to me. I could see that my pemphigus was drying up a bit. But my face looked old and tired; my eyes had rings under them from fatigue. I could only stare at my reflection, at the shock of gray hair, the blue eyes and high cheekbones, the unequally clefted chin, the wrinkles, the ugly masses of drying, postulant lesions, and I felt as if I was looking at a death's-head.

I got into the hot, steaming shower, which seemed to help clear my head. And as it did, I felt afraid. If Mengele was actually here, then I had given myself over to him. I had gone back to him to die, giving *him* the satisfaction.

I had wanted to find Mengele to vindicate my life.

I had wanted to kill him.

That had been the purpose of my life.

But instead I had become a prisoner again...sick and weak, and in no position to kill anyone.

I didn't even know where I was, or how long I had been here. If this room was any example, I was in a house the size of a castle.

How could such a place exist unknown in the jungle?

Was I even *in* the jungle?

Or was I still in the clearing, drugged-out and dreaming...?

* * * * * * *

I dressed quickly in the fresh clothes that the Indian laid out for me. Everything fit well: the trousers, shirt, and jacket, all of which felt to be silk. I was even provided with a tie, which was dark blue and flecked with red.

"What's your name?" I asked the Indian.

"Gata," he said. "You are feeling well?"

I nodded. Surprisingly, I did feel well. "Where is this place?"

"You will come with me and the *Doutor* will talk to you."

"Why can't you talk to me?"

"The *Doutor* will explain everything," and then he made an odd *hnrung, hnrung* noise. I couldn't determine if he was laughing or clearing his throat.

Before we left the room, he looked around, as if he might have forgotten something; and then walked over to an eight-legged ebony *pietre dure* chest that looked to be seventeenth century Italian, and opened one of the drawers, which was inlaid with light wood. "This is yours," he said and handed me my pistol. I was dumbfounded, but I checked it: it was loaded.

"Why are you giving me this?" I asked.

"It is yours, is it not? You told me you wanted to kill the *Doutor*. You don't seem strong enough to kill him with your hands."

"Do you *want* me to kill him?" I asked, incredulous, but he ignored my question. I laid the pistol down on a side table; but he picked it up, handed it back to me, and then motioned me to leave the room, which let out into a wide, dark hallway.

I shook my head, tucked the pistol into my belt, and buttoned my jacket. We walked quickly down the hallway, Gata keeping a tight grip on my arm, our feet padding on the carpet. I could hear the soft whoosh of air and feel a thrumming, which was probably air-conditioning, for without it, the plush carpets we were walking on would be wet with mould.

"You must tell me what is going on. Where are we going?" I asked again. I followed him down a flight of stairs. "Well...? I asked, but he ignored me. It seemed we were in another wing of the house, but there were no windows in the halls. The carpet was all the same color: a gray so dark it was almost black. He stopped beside a door that was partially open, but all I could see of the room were dark paneled walls and bookshelves. Then I turned to ask Gata a question, but he was gone, as if he had vanished. It was a cheap stunt and I was frustrated and suddenly angry, especially since I *knew* that I would have noticed him walking away. He had virtually disappeared.

He must have stepped into the doorway behind me.

I was debating whether I should try to find my way

out of here and look for Genaro when a white haired man appeared at the doorway and gestured me inside. He walked across a parquet floor of inlaid circles and triangles and sat down behind what looked to be an early eighteenth century partner's desk. It was ebony and bare, except for some papers, an ashtray, and a computer monitor. I followed him into the room, slowly, my heart pounding in my throat, my hands shaking, and I could feel myself sweating. Although I had just bathed, my illness seemed to be working like an engine again, pushing sweat out of my pores. In those first seconds, I seemed to be seeing everything at once, hundreds of details, and, as if in a dream, everything took on equal weight: primitive bronze sculptures in the window bays; a folio stand filled with etchings, the topmost a Goya grotesque; a large crystal chandelier that was brightly lit, as if in a cloud of soft yellow; a breakfront bookcase with leather-bound volumes; an expanse of library shelves on the wall opposite the desk, all available space filled with paperbacks and hardcovers, stacked every which way, and between them, grotesque curiosities: gray plaster casts of arms with clenched fists, legs, and various animal limbs, and brightly colored marquetry boxes and crystal cones and spheres; another shelf was lined with carved wooden heads, one of which I recognized: Mengele, the young Mengele I had known; and the old man himself, staring at me from behind his desk, the shadow of a smile caught on his face, and those were the same blue eyes I had looked into forty years ago; I could see the space between his front teeth—the wrinkles and walrus mustache and shadows under his deeply set eyes couldn't hide him.

It was indeed Mengele. It could have been any gentle looking old man, but I knew it wasn't. And as if he had remembered me, impossible though it might be, he spoke to me in a soft voice; he spoke to me in German. "Sit down," he said, indicating the caned armchair before his desk. He lit a cigarette, blowing out the smoke without inhaling it.

"You *are* Mengele," I said, standing before him.

"Yes."

And as I stood there, having found him after all the years of searching, I couldn't say a word. I looked into his eyes and remembered the death's head held up by the coroner at the cemetery in Embu, I remembered faces I had not thought about since I'd left the camps, and they appeared before my eyes in succession, flashing past me, my friends and acquaintances that Mengele had killed, and once again I felt the presence of my mother, just as I had with the whore in Manaus; I felt as if her atoms were floating in the air, yellowish motes of skin and bone, light as hair, emanating from the chandelier above. The room seemed to be getting smaller. I felt dizzy and was overwhelmed by a deep oceanic sadness. It was as if the room was filled with it, as if Mengele, this old man who had outwitted the world, exuded it.

He had murdered my mother; for him it was a small thing of no consequence, a nod of his head. Hadn't he gassed six hundred women so he could disinfect their barracks for typhus; it was more effectual to kill them than move them.

And I remembered my dream of David, my brother, remembered asking Mengele to electrocute *him* instead of me.

But he had killed David.

Just as he had killed me.

I found my voice and trembling with anger, I said, "I watched them exhume your grave."

"Yes," he said. "I read about that."

"Are you saying you knew nothing about it?"

"No, of course not. I set it up. The Bosserts and most of the other people involved knew nothing, though; they, too, thought I had really died. The search for Mengele is over." He looked at me, his gaze steady, unnerving, but I returned it in kind. My bones would have to shatter before he would have the best of me again. His gaze gave me strength, for in it I rediscovered my hatred of him, for his eyes were like mirrors of the past, my past. In them I saw my mother and brother, trapped in death without vindication.

In them I saw myself.

"I know who you are," Mengele said. "I saw that in your dream when you took the drug."

"And how did you do that?" I asked, and I opened my jacket and took out the pistol Gata had given me. I had lived out my life for this assassination. First him, then me. Only I would give myself up to the rot of my disease; not to Mengele. At least there would be that.

If I was going to kill him, it had to be now, before he answered my questions, before something or someone interfered, before he could talk me into letting him live. I aimed the gun at his face, and as I did so, I felt cold and numb, my thoughts bits of ice, and I was a machine once again. As in childhood, I was a mechanical thing, a motor that propelled itself around the camps with little or no fuel, a dead thing of flesh and bone that had only the gift of motion, whose emotions and thoughts were cold and glacial, never to completely thaw.

"Thank you," he said, smiling benignly. "Thank you, but it won't work."

I pulled the trigger, squeezing it, and felt a slight shock to my arm. The noise didn't startle me. It was as if I was deaf, as if this whole event was taking place in slow motion.

Mengele continued to stare at me, even as the bullet tore through his forehead, a neat hole immediately pouring blood down his nose and cheeks, a wash of bright red. It was as if he was looking into me, as the death's-head skull had at Embu, looking into my memories, my failure, my being.

I fired again and again, turning his face and neck into blood, bone, and butcher's meat. But not in defense. Not this time. This time *I* was the storm and the thunder. This time *I* was the dispatcher, God, taking and giving life, the needle and the knife.

I was Mengele, calm as death, as the everlasting.

But I felt no vindication, no release. Only cold, as if I had been dropped into a sea of Onca's numbing gruel.

And then once again I felt the thud of a blunt object across the back of my head, and the radiant whiteness, fading, fading....

* * * * * * *

I regained consciousness in the bedroom where I had found myself before. It was dark, but I could make out the outlines of objects in the room, objects I had seen but not noticed: the bric-a-brac in the bookshelves, the gilt-edged picture frames on the walls, the foot-posts of the bed, heavy window drapes, a large table covered with books. And I could make out the shape of someone in a stuffed chair across the room. I listened, but couldn't even make out his—or her—breathing. Just the outside noises, which were damped, as if the world had been muffled. Then the pain closed over me, as if it had somehow been forgotten in my first seconds of waiting, but broke through, to make itself known. I first felt an aching in my arm, as if it were terribly bruised, and then—as someone just coming out of anesthesia from an operation and trying to sort out the different parts of his anatomy in order to reconstruct himself back to awareness—I realized that pain was shooting through my stomach, chest, head, my entire body. I groaned, and the shadow in the chair rose and walked over to my bed.

It was Genaro.

He parted the netting on the bed and picked up a syringe in a plastic container from my night table. He inserted the needle into the rubber top of a small glass bottle and drew a measured amount of the reddish liquid into the syringe.

"Genaro, how long have you been here?" I asked. "And what the hell are you giving me?"

"Medicine," he said. And he injected me in the thigh. I hardly felt it. "You've been in bed for over a week. Are you feeling any better, Meester?"

"No," I said.

"Do you have the *diarrhea*?"

"No—I don't know. How could I have been here for over a week. It's been a day and a night, I think. What was that medication you gave me, and where were you before?"

You always ask two things at once, Meester," Genaro said. He expertly broke the disposable syringe needle and dropped it into a plastic lined garbage can beside the bed.

"The medicine...."

"You have been getting different kinds of medicine."

"What kinds?" I asked.

"To make you well."

"Cut the bullshit, Genaro. What did you just give me?"

"A medicine something like the one you inhaled before. Do you remember that?"

"That was a hallucinogen, what the hell are you giving me that for?" I tried to sit up, but my head hurt so much I had to remain where I was."

"No," Genaro said, "it will all make you better. Touch your face, go ahead, Meester. Do you see, the pimples are gone."

I felt for the lesions and, indeed, they seemed to have disappeared.

"This drug," Genaro continued, "it is very strong, which is why you feel the pain."

I could feel it working through my bloodstream, an injection of icy liquid freezing my arteries and veins. As I looked up at Genaro, I saw another face super-imposed upon his, a ghostly, evanescent apparition, which disappeared and reappeared like the neon that was blinking on and off in that room in Manaus. As the drug began to turn my face and eyes cold, I could make out who Genaro really was.

He was the Indian who had given me the drug.

He was an old man. A young man.

He had taken me to Mengele.

I had killed Mengele. The remembrance and realiza-tion was a shock. But it was not true, not real. It was a set-up. It was too easy, too pat.

"You are not Genaro," I said.

"I am, Meester. I am...."

"You are the Indian."

"I am both. Only now you can see that."

"And Mengele, you know about that?"

"You killed him, but he is not dead."

"Then it's *all* hallucination."

"No," Genaro said. "It's real, but like a play."

"Was that Mengele, then, or you?"

Genaro made the hnrung sound, then said, "It was not me."

"How do you know what happened?"

"I see into you, just as the *Doutor* does."

"How?"

"He will tell you that...tomorrow."

"Or next week, if you keep me drugged—"

"Tomorrow we will leave this room and you will see this place."

"And Mengele."

"And Mengele," he repeated. "But now you must sleep."

"Is *this* my dream?"

"It is and it isn't," Genaro said. "We are all in it together. I will show you tomorrow."

"Will you stay here tonight?"

He smiled, the old side of his face not as flexible as the young and thus grimacing, said, "Yes, Meester, I will stay and watch you lose the cancer."

I heard his words, but they seemed to hang in the darkness, frozen, just as I was, turned to glass by the injection of hallucinogens.

CHAPTER NINE
GEOMETRY

Tomorrow....

I awakened in a blaze of light. My head ached and throbbed with it. My eyes, blinded by retinal afterimages, were squeezed shut; but the light seemed to know no boundaries. It was outside and inside, and I was burning with it.

"Come on, now, Meester, you have slept quite enough."

I opened my eyes, expecting to be looking into the sun, expecting Genaro to be beside me, tending me. Instead, I found Mengele sitting and smoking a cigarette in the stuffed chair across the room; the fragrant odor of Turkish tobacco suffused the air. Mengele was dressed in a tan linen suit, and he smiled at me, as if I were a source of great pride to him.

Light streamed in through the windows, illuminating white tendrils of smoke that seemed to dance and swirl and curl in the air. The heavy brocade curtains were open, but the room itself was cool and shadowed. I blinked, still seeing afterimages, as if I had indeed been staring into bright light, as if I were still seeing the outlines of dreams. My skin burned, tingled. "Where is Genaro?"

"He left some weeks ago," Mengele said, speaking to me in German.

I sat up in bed. I was wearing satin pajamas. Everything smelled fresh, clean, healthy. Perfumed. "He told me that he would wait...."

He promised....

Mengele nodded. "He waited to see that you were well. He administrated to you and sent the nurse away. Then, when you were out of danger, he came to me. He gave the dreams back to me, the dreams that made him double. Old like me and young like you." He smiled again, as if enjoying the irony of calling me young.

"What did you do to him?"

"Long ago he was sick, and I helped him. Like he helped you." Smiling through smoke. "Like we helped you. Now, thanks to my generosity, he is free. All debts paid, and so he has gone back to his heavy-fleshed wife and to your burned land." Mengele stood up. "But you and I...we have each other's poison, and we have Genaro's poison. So what shall we do with all these poisonous nightmares? What shall we do?" He gave me a paternalistic look, tapped the carved wooden arm of the chair, and then stood up. He had the energy of a young man. "Now get dressed and meet me in the garden. You are no longer ill, except for the sickness in your soul. Are you hungry?"

I took a deep breath and realized that my stomach didn't hurt, my body didn't ache—the headache had dissolved—and indeed I was suddenly famished. I nodded, and he bowed and left the room. A moment later a pregnant woman brought me a tray of food: bacon and eggs, manioc, and cubes of barely cooked meat. She set the tray on the bed and stepped back while I ate.

She wore a rough skirt, but no blouse; her heavy breasts were splayed and painted with thick red circles and scallops. She had a wide, child-like face, and her heavy earlobes were pierced with wooden plugs; balsa spokes radiated from her nasal septum, giving her the appearance of a heavy, pregnant cat.

"Are you my nurse?" I asked in Portuguese, then in English and German; but she didn't respond. She just stood near the bed and waited until I was finished; then she took the tray and left me to dress.

I got out of bed and suddenly felt a rush of joy. I wasn't dizzy. I felt weak, but not ill. I was going to live. I was on fire, but I was going to live.

I gazed out the window at Mengele's formal maze of a garden and saw Mengele below, patiently waiting for me.

* * * * * * *

We walked a straight line through Mengele's tropical gardens, which for all the wild, exotic growth were formal and studied: expansive lawns that directed the eye to stone steps, classically inspired fountains, huge sculpted topiaries, arbors and enclosures with geometer's lines of miraculous tropical color—planned and limited explosions of shrub, vine, and flowers—pergolas, bowers, streams, ponds, and angel white temples. Surrounding all was rain forest, the ominous dark green walls that appeared to extend forever.

Behind us was his neoclassical mansion of red brick, white marble, and hundreds of oblong windows, a house that would have suited Jane Austen's England, but was a red welt here in this land of lush growth.

"I told you it wouldn't work," Mengele said as we walked down a mown path toward an open Ionic temple.

I had a fleeting thought that the temple was a doorway into a dangerous yet magical forest. "What wouldn't work?" I asked.

"Murdering me."

"So I see." I studied his face, looking for Uncle Pepe, the younger, hard-faced Mengele.

"Oh, I'm dead all right, just like Erwin Schrödinger's cat." Mengele kept a brisk pace, as if he had created this garden for marching rather than strolling. Do you know about that?"

"Yes," I said impatiently. But—"

"In Schrödinger's thought experiment, the cat is alive in one universe, dead in another. It all depends on the observer whether he sees a live cat or a dead one."

"Well, I guess I just picked the wrong universe."

"No," my son, "you are between them. You have not made your choice yet."

"How do you know that?"

Mengele made the hnrung, hnrung sound, the

mocking sound of the dreamer.

"Well...?" I asked.

"Because I have made *my* choice." He seemed pleased with himself. "It gives one a certain perspective and advantage."

"Let me guess," I said. "You choose to live."

"You will know that soon enough, too," Mengele said as he stepped between the columns of the temple, his feet clattering on the tiled stone floor."

"Where are you taking me?"

"For a walk. Are you tired?"

"A bit."

"Then I know just the place where we can rest," and Mengele crossed the floor of the temple, stepped onto the lawn on the other side, and directed me to follow him into the rainforest. The demarcation between garden and forest could have been drawn with a straightedge; it certainly wasn't natural. "It must take an army of gardeners to keep the rainforest from taking over," I said.

"No, the trees stop just there of their own accord." Mengele gazed at me as if I was a child again, his expression gentle, his eyes guileless and clear as the empty sky above; and once again I noticed the gap between his front teeth and the mole on his left cheek. "I've learned to live in harmony with nature," Mengele said.

As we walked under a canopy of evenly spaced trees, the temperature dropped, the world darkened; and then we were in the rainforest. Everything was quiet, hushed, as if we had entered a cathedral. The light was soft and weak; shadows danced across the columns of trees. Mengele slowed his pace and appeared to relax. I felt a sudden, cold apprehension that something palpable had changed, or would change. Light flickered through branches; little black uakaris monkeys leaped through the foliage high above, shaking the fronds; parrots screeched; and, distracted, I almost stepped on a small, crimson snake that corkscrewed into the thick leaf mulch. Everything seemed to be in sudden movement; and just as suddenly we stepped into a large clearing. I could feel the heat of the late-morning sun on my face. The ground was cracked; half-charred tree stumps were everywhere. I could see a large thatch-roofed hut on the other side of the clearing, the soil seemingly fertile around it, for there were plenty of fruit trees: orange, lemon, plum, and mango; and coconut and cashew nut and breadfruit. I could also hear water in the distance, a great roaring; perhaps a waterfall. As we neared the hut, I saw that the walls were constructed of closely placed palings. There were no windows—that would certainly keep out the mosquitoes—only a door covered with thatch. A woman in her fifties was roasting manioc in an open shelter a few yards from the hut. She was naked from the waist up like my nurse, her body chalked and dyed to resemble the markings of a jaguar, her nose and lips festooned with palm splinters, She shook a square pan and raked the grains back and forth with a stick. "Whoooo," she shouted, alerting whoever was in the hut, and grinned happily at Mengele. Mengele said something to her in her own tongue, which she seemed to find hysterically funny; and then he gestured to me to follow him into the hut. Someone inside the hut screamed, a strangled scream that chilled me.

The woman smiled at Mengele and shook her head sharply as we went inside.

It was dark and close and fetid: the smells of illness, perspiration, kerosene, smoke, and something else, something sweet and cloying. Several lanterns hung from support posts and cast a reddish light. A fire was burning, the resinous smoke rising. Beside the fire a woman was lying upon a pallet. A man leaned over her, drew noisily upon a hand-rolled cigarette, and blew the smoke into the woman's face. As my eyes adjusted to the murky darkness, I could make out more and more details. The woman was white, blond, in her thirties, perhaps; but emaciated, ravaged. Her cheeks were sunken, and she was wheezing with every breath; her eyes stared blindly ahead.

The man looked at Mengele, questioning. His dark features were flattened, his thick black hair combed over his forehead. He could have been thirty or sixty; I couldn't tell. He wore a red and blue-checked shirt and white rumpled trousers.

"Bom dia, doutor."

"It is going well, Báquiro?" Mengele asked.

"This woman is very sick. She has too many darts inside her. All over. In her liver. In her stomach. In her head. Her eyes are nearly dead, so it is very hard to see the darts. Where they are."

Mengele nodded, then sat down on a pallet. I followed suit. "Báquiro, this is Stephen."

Báquiro nodded to me. *"Aprendiz?"* he asked Mengele.

Mengele laughed, and I felt hot anger constricting my chest. "I'm not anybody's apprentice." I started to stand up, but Mengele gently tapped my knee. "Báquiro is very special, very talented. He is a *brujo*, a doctor who helps me. And he is also a great herbalist. He believes that spirits or demons or perhaps another *brujo* has shot invisible darts into his patient. Those darts made her ill and will kill her...or so Báquiro believes."

"And you?" I asked.

"Are you asking if I believe in Báquiro's invisible dart etiology?"

Mengele just smiled at me.

"I go back into her now," Báquiro said, and he leaned close to her, looking into her dead eyes, as if to brush his lips against hers, a quiet foreplay. The image of a snake about to strike formed in my mind.

"Her mother brought her here to me," Mengele said. He chuckled. "The trek almost killed both of them."

"Why did you bring *me* here?" I asked.

"To rest, of course, and to show you miracles."

"I thought you believed yourself to be a man of science."

"I have always been a man of science, Stephen. Then as now I believed in transformation."

"No, you believed in murder."

"I believed in healing," Mengele said, "but I was an agent of the state, the community...the volk."

"Curing by killing, is that it?"

Mengele gazed at the *brujo* and his dying, blond patient.

"I was a physician-biologist. I believed in National Socialism, which, in essence, was applied biology. I believed the volk was the vessel of God; I was nothing but one of its instruments."

"And now? Now that there is no volk to give you an excuse to murder?"

Mengele smiled and shook his head, a slight, subtle movement. "You are right, Stephen, the volk is now history, and so I have moved on. I came here, to this place of ignorance, to do what I can. To cure whom I can."

"Just as you cured the Jews, just as you cured my brother and my mother?" The mephitic closeness of the hut seemed to dampen voice and emotion; I spoke to Mengele as if I was separated by a great distance, yet we could hear each other's every whisper...every breath and heartbeat.

"Much that happened was unfortunate," Mengele said as he watched Báquiro, who was leaning over the sick woman as if giving her mouth-to-mouth resuscitation. "I was indeed trying to cure. Our mission was nothing less than the remaking of the German people and, in time, the people of the world. That was the mission of all doctors who were adherents of National Socialism. Our focus was revitalization and purification. But you were our misfortune. Our disease. The camps tested us all. Every killing went against the grain, but it had to be done; and we had to be hard. There was no choice. It was a war of racial hygiene. We were trying to save humanity."

"From me," I said, goading him.

"Yes, from all of you."

"You can't still believe that."

"No," Mengele said. "Of course not. It was a long time ago. The world has changed, we have changed."

"No, we haven't changed."

"Ah, but yes we have, Stephen. I can still believe in my unfortunate past and live in the present. I cured you, after all."

"Why?"

He smiled. "I suppose old habits die hard. I still believe in saving humanity."

"But I am *still* a Jew." That meant to incite.

Mengele looked over at me, then back at Báquiro. "It is only a slight shift in definition, Stephen. You have what we used to call hardness. You have always been a good soldier, or have you forgotten what you did to my old comrade Rudolf Heninger?"

I took a deep breath. Yes, I remembered. I had bludgeoned the executioner of Riga to death.

"You did what you did, and now he lives within you, doesn't he? Just as those poor unfortunates I have killed live within me." He smiled. "And just as I live within you."

"*Doutor*," Báquiro said, and his voice seemed to

shatter the atmosphere; I felt as if someone had awakened me from painful dream-blasted sleep. "Do you and your *aprendiz* wish to help me, or to leave?"

Mengele glanced at me, and I nodded.

"What do you wish us to do," he asked Báquiro.

"You must help her to sit up," Báquiro said, "and you"—he pointed to me by raising his head—"you will please stand by the doorway in case the mother returns. She is of a strong mind, and my Maquichemi will not be able to keep her away."

I assumed Maquichemi was the woman we met outside the hut.

And so I stood by the doorway, waited and watched. I could hear Maquichemi shuffling around outside, talking and singing to herself, could hear the distant roaring of water and the machine cawing of birds. Inside, it was close and humid and had become stiflingly, impossibly hot. My shirt was plastered to my wet skin, my eyes burned, yet Báquiro stoked the fire, as if he needed more and more heat to melt the imaginary darts inside his dying patient. I considered pulling the canvass away from the hut's opening and taking a breath of fresh air. The smoke in the hut was palpable; I could taste it, dry and acrid on the tongue; but there was something else in the air, something besides burning wood and sweat and the whiff of turpentine, something sweet that reminded me of rancid meat and roses.

I had smelled it all too often before. It was the sick smell of death.

Báquiro chanted and prayed, and then gave directions to Mengele.

"Now you will blow some darts into me, *Doutor*, and then I will blow them into the mouth of the woman." He directed himself to his patient. "*Senhora* Bonpland, can you hear me?" The woman sat on the floor, her back braced against a post, her eyes glazed; she nodded. "Good. I am going to give you *veneno*, good poison to chase away the bad poison inside you. And my good friend will give me the poison. Are you prepared?"

She did not respond.

Báquiro unbuttoned her blouse and daubed and smeared red onoto seed dye on her forehead, temples, stomach, breasts, and the area of her liver and kidneys.

"Each spot indicates darts, indicates *veneno*, disease...."

Then he walked to the end of the hut, removed two open-work baskets from a pole stuck high in the thatch, and pulled the pole free. The pole was a two foot long reed cane pipe. He examined its tarry black nozzle and picked through the contents of one of the baskets until he found a coffee jar filled with brown powder, which he carefully poured into the nozzle. After tapping the pipe to distribute the drug, he walked over to his patient, kneeled beside her, and motioned to Mengele to do the same. He offered one end of the pipe to Mengele and said, "Now you must blow the poison into me. You must take a deep breath and blow very hard. After that, you must not help me or the woman."

Mengele nodded.

"And you, Meester *Aprendiz*," he said, looking at me with his hard face and deeply set dark eyes, "you must guard the door. But you will see everything as if you too have the poison." He grinned at me, then at Mengele, and put the end of the reed pipe into his left nostril. "*Agora*," he said to Mengele.

And Mengele blew the contents of the tube into Báquiro's nose, a terrific blast.

I felt that blast and staggered backward; for an instant, it seemed that the hut was suddenly filled with burning, coruscating light.

Báquiro coughed and spat, and then instructed Mengele to insert one end of the pipe into Senhora Bonpland's nose. Mengele did so; and when Báquiro blew into the tube, Senhora Bonpland jerked backward as if she had been kicked in the face. She banged her head on the pole, and her nose began to bleed. She looked directly at me, terrified, her head jerking as she strained for breath that would not come.

"Spit out the darts," Báquiro shouted; he clapped his hands. "Spit them out." But the woman could only make gagging sounds. Her skin color began to change. Báquiro pulled her to her feet and holding her from behind, he squeezed her sternum, as if he were performing the Heimlich maneuver. She coughed, then took a wheezing deep breath and, her gaze still locked on mine—although I had no idea if she could actually *see* me—she exhaled, coughing up the poison.

Surely I was dreaming because I could *see* the darts,

ethereal as ectoplasm, leave her mouth and eyes, the darts discharged, coming toward me as if shot from a bow, the darts poisonous and compact, slivers of hate and despair and grief, crystal hard shards of Mengele's Nazi hardness.

My mind, like a stop motion camera, recording.

Báquiro grinning.

Mengele now helping Báquiro hold *Senhora* Bonpland upright.

Senhora Bonpland gazing at me. Her face slack. Her eyes wide with recognition. Perhaps *I* am the brujo....

The darts the radiant crystal whiteness flying, piercing, piercing, then fading....

Transforming me.

Waking me once again to nightmare.

* * * * * * *

"So that was your idea of taking me to a place where I could rest," I said to Mengele as we walked back through the rainforest, through the twilight corridors and rooms defined by great boles of trees.

Mengele smiled, obviously enjoying the sarcasm.

"Well, Stephen, are you not rested?"

"I am in pain...and I am still dreaming," I said, looking around at a pair of orange winged parrots that seemed to fluoresce and glitter like jewels caught in bright light. My chest ached and burned, as if indeed I had been struck by darts. My lungs felt constricted, phlegmy; my breathing was ragged. I could hear thunder, resounding rolling thunder, but the pelting rain of the storm above could not pierce the tangled canopy of the forest, which also radiated its own crystalline light, as if some impossible ice storm had turned every bole and branch, every fern and palm into shimmering, living glass. "You are doing this."

Mengele laughed. "You believe that I am creating all that you see around you?"

"Yes," I said. "Are you going to tell me it is real?"

"Of course it is real," Mengele said.

"You don't believe it is a dream?"

"Why should it matter what I believe? But, yes, it is a dream and, yes, it is real. Actually it is two dreams, probably more. Didn't your servant tell you that dreams talk to each other?"

I didn't respond, but, indeed, Genaro's fleshy wife Onca had told me that.

We walked through the demarcation that separated rain forest from Mengele's estate, walked through pouring rain along his expansive, manicured lawns to the shelter of his Ionic temple. The grass was steaming; we were soaked.

"You said you were in pain from the darts," Mengele said.

"Yes."

"So am I...."

And with that everything but the rain disappeared.

* * * * * * *

My head ached, my ears were ringing from the cacophony all around me, and I found myself standing on the selection ramp in Auschwitz. I needed a drink. It was dark and cold, slushy rain flew through the air, and the sky was blacked out as if by a velvet curtain. But there were miles of lights, glittering Christmas lights strung in geometric patterns. To my right in the distance was the only star in the sky, a stinking, flesh-melting beacon of light: the flame of the crematorium. Auschwitz's own eternal lamp. Directly ahead of me, a freight train steamed on the track. The doors of the boxcars were being slid open by S. S. guards directed by Ernst Jäckel, the *Arbeitsführer*, who stood beside me on the platform.

But I was in charge.

Or rather Mengele was in charge.

I tried to wake myself from his dream his memory his past his life, but I couldn't. I was in Mengele's dream, and in that dream I was Mengele. Mengele dressed in a freshly laundered black SS uniform: black jodhpurs, spit-shined riding boots. His face was recently shaved; he smelled of soap and perfume; he was the epitome of scoured cleanliness, and I remembered the aphorism *cleanliness is next to godliness*, but was that Mengele's memory or my own? I couldn't tell. He stood ramrod straight and tall, the picture of dignified military bearing, and inhaled the familiar odors of unclean flesh, urine, and feces wafting around him. Not even the rain could cleanse the stink, which was augmented by the foul sick sweet exhalations of the crematorium.

But I was used to it...hardened to it.

I shouted at Jäckel's men to hurry up, to get the damn Jews out of the trains and into order, to line them up into columns of five; and the guards, in turn, shouted "*Raus, raus, raus.*" They shot those prisoners who could not disembark from the boxcars quickly enough; and the rest of the Jews rushed out of the cars, fell and slipped in the mud, looked around frantically for means of escape, but there was none: Only walls and high barb-wire fences. Alsatian guard dogs barked and snapped, biting hard into flesh and bone. SS guards rounded up the skeletal old men in filthy jackets, the elderly women wearing *scheitel* wigs, the children with their mothers, the young men and women, the fathers, mothers, cousins, neighbors...the doctors, lawyers, and rabbis, the accountants and artists, the carpenters, butchers, and plumbers, all wearing their defining yellow *Juden* stars.

It occurred to me that the guards hurrying in constant awkward skittering jarring motion were dogs themselves; but they did their work, and I began selecting those prisoners who would be saved to work and those who would be transported to the gas chambers in the Red Cross trucks idling nearby. I would save those I could, but what matter if the poor wretches croaked in shit or ascended to Heaven in a cloud of gas?

I slapped my riding crop against my gloved right hand and paced back and forth...selecting. So many faces, a sea of faces. But to me they were nothing more than shadows, wraiths; and I was but an actor in a shadow box play. I was efficient, however. I was proud of the speed and efficiency of my selections. There was no need for two doctors when I stood on the ramp.

I said *"links"*—*"left"*—and the guards removed a family to the waiting trucks. I said *"rechts"*—*"right"*—and the guards directed a young beautiful Jewess to wait with the other Jews who would live for a little while longer.

"Links."

"Rechts."

Ten people, twenty people, thirty people selected. I was a metronome, setting the time for a sort of monstrous, mythic music.

Forty, fifty, sixty, one hundred.

"Links." "Rechts." "Links." "Rechts."

Two hundred.

When his turn came, a malingerer with a bulging forehead and suppurating sores on his face pleaded for light work. I directed him to the left and told him that indeed he'll get light work where he's going. A woman who didn't want to be separated from her mother and sister tried to force her way past a guard. The guard was distracted and let her pass, but I stopped her myself. When she tried to scratch me, I struck her hard in the face and directed her back to her own group. Selection was a precise procedure. This woman had been chosen to live and work. Her mother was too old to work; her sister too young. They would only succumb to illness and die. Better the gas.

One of the Jäckel's guards fired into the horde.

A woman wearing so many ragged clothes that one

couldn't discern her figure screamed "Hershel" and fell on top of the dead man.

"Stop the noise," I shouted at the guard. "You will *not* shoot unless I so order...or unless your *Arbeitsführer* so orders." I glanced at Ernst Jäckel, who bowed his head slightly in respect: My relations with all the camp staff were always based on mutual respect. But as the woman continued to scream, I ordered her shot to maintain order in the ranks. I leaned toward Ernst and reminded him that his men needed to be looking for twins. He instructed his men, and the shout went up—

"Zwillinge raus!"

"Twins out!"

"Zwillinge heraustreten!"

"Twins step forward!"

"Twins will receive special treatment!"

"Twins will be safe!"

"Step forward *now* and identify yourselves!"

And thus I received a miracle: a set of light-skinned, blond twin boys. I picked them up, gave them each a squeeze and a cuddle. One of the little boys cried for his mother. I cuddled him again and whispered in his ear.

"Wilst du die Schnauze halten?"

"Why don't you shut your mouth?"

Understanding that I would take care of him, the little angel stopped crying. As I passed the boy over to one of the striped suited prisoner workers for safekeeping, the twin's mother looked up at me. She begged and pleaded with me to allow her to remain with her children. She was nothing but a brittle, shivering, brown-haired phantom. Rags and bones.

I nodded, encouraged her not to worry, and off to the left she went.

It was the humane option. Sooner or later they must all go to the gas. So if it were to be done, best it were done now with speed and mercy. Selections would always be difficult, for the selection of life unworthy of life was the consummate battlefield test of will, temper, sacrifice, and *hardness*.

Now that I had found my twins, I relaxed. The test of selection became comfortably pro forma. A monotony of *links rechts links rechts*. The cold settled in, numbing, and I was the metronome ticking off life and death, the true metronome measuring and regulating the truest, purest, most wrathful and mathematically elegant music ever composed.

"*Links Rechts Links Rechts*."

I was Moses parting this sea of corrupted souls.

A prisoner came forward and with great hesitation told me that he was a doctor. Once I ascertained that he was properly credentialed—he was an ophthalmologist; and I was very pleased, as I had specific research in mind with which he could assist me—I welcomed the reticent Dr. Erich Bostroem. I explained to him that the prisoner physicians who work in my research facilities receive better rations and lodging than all other prisoners and are engaged in important medical work, cutting-edge experimentation and research. I invited him to keep me company while I continued my selections, and I asked the *Arbeitsführer* to make sure that all doctors were singled out so that Dr. Bostroem and I could decide if they would be selected to work with me in the hospital.

As I made my selections, my new colleague shivered beside me.

The hours passed slowly, even with the companionship of another doctor. I didn't hate him because he was a Jew, because he was as dirty and ill-smelling as the others I was selecting. I was in a life and death struggle to purify the blood, a life and death struggle with the Jewish race. Jews were a formidable foe and highly gifted. Nevertheless they were a lower race, and the only cure for the world was their annihilation. But for this short time on this cold, rainy morning, Dr. Bostroem and I constructed a truce. For these few moments or hours, I would accord him the professional respect that was his due, and he would regail me with his ophthalmologic expertise. Indeed, we selected a number of prisoner doctors, saving them for the time being; and Dr. Bostroem stood in place and shivered as I made general selections.

"How can you make these...determinations so quickly?" he asked.

I had no intention of validating such a question. Nor did he slow me down. I continued to select, even as I explained some of the work I was doing that might be within his professional purview. I told him I was conducting research on the heredity factors of heterochromia. "In six of eight Gypsy twins, we found the occurrence of heterochromia. Each had one blue eye and one brown eye."

Dr. Bostroem nodded, obviously interested.

"I've had the eyes transported to Berlin for further study," I continued.

Dr. Bostroem disapproved. He started to shake his head, but regained control over himself. He would soon learn that his place was not to approve...or disapprove.

"No, no," I shouted at a guard who was directing a family into the wrong line.

As I continued selecting, I explained a project I had in mind for Dr. Bostroem. "I have several prisoners, Jews and Gypsies, that have heterochromia. They also have syphilis and tuberculosis, which is not optimal. I have theorized that by injecting methylene blue into their eyes, we might change the color. I would like you to direct the project. I will provide you with proper facilities tomorrow morning. You can then prepare a list of anything else you might need."

"But why would you wish to do such a thing?" he asked.

Without thought, I lifted the *scheitel* wig from an old woman's head with my riding crop; it was like picking a scab. It was the fascination of the abominable, the ugly, and reprehensible. Dr. Bostroem made a noise deep in his throat, and perhaps it was the cold and the hour—first light—that caught me because I, too, lost control for an instant and asked, Would *you* like to take over the selections, Doctor?"

"Dr. Bostroem apologized.

I nodded, and then asked him to make a selection.

"To the right or to the left, which will it be Dr. Bostroem?"

Faltering. "To the right."

I nodded again, and waved the old woman off to be sent to the camp where she would surely expire in a matter of days.

"And my husband," she cried. "He, too...."

A watery-eyed, skinny old man held onto her hand as if he were drowning."

"Well?" I asked the doctor.

He nodded.

"*Rechts.*"

But I made the next selection myself.

I sent Dr. Bostroem to the crematorium.

The truce was over.

* * * * * * *

Moments, hours, or an eternity later, I staggered backward as a blast of burning, coruscating light blinded me; and then the blessed weight of total, numbing, humane darkness suffocated me.

Snuffed me out like a candle.

CHAPTER TEN
THE DETERMINISM OF DARKNESS

When I awoke, I was back in Mengele's house, lying in a four-poster bed.

I looked up at the gauzy mosquito netting, listened to the high-pitched whirring of occasional insects, and breathed deeply. My heart was beating wildly. Surely it was the dream, the nightmare somehow waking me up in the midst of REM sleep. I was lying on top of the embroidered snow white coverlet. I was dressed in the same slacks and shirt I had worn to accompany Mengele into the rainforest. I was unwashed and sweaty, my hair was greasy, and I stank of wood smoke and something else: the faint smell of ash. I sat up, half-expecting Mengele to be sitting and smoking in the stuffed chair across the room. I called for Gata, Mengele's aide—or was he Mengele's servant? He was the half young half old Indian who had given me the drug when I was in the rainforest with Genaro; and I remembered that when I was ill and feverish and lit with force-fed hallucinogens, I had imagined that Gata and Genaro were somehow one and the same. Superimposed, one over the other.

I called for my nurse, the bare breasted Indian woman with the wide face and heavy body painted in red circles. But I was alone. I could hear distant voices, but could not make them out. I shuddered, remembering my nightmare of being Mengele, remembering how it felt to *be* Mengele, to stand on the ramp in Auschwitz and select Jews and gypsies for death; and even now, I could remember all the details of Mengele's personal and private past, a lifetime of details. I could remember his memories as if they were my own.

I panicked and ran to the bathroom to make sure it would be my face staring out at me from the mirror. Indeed, it was my face, not Mengele's; my face without a mark of the wild fire, the pemphigus that had disfigured it. Although I was exhausted and cotton-mouthed, I felt strong and healthy. The cancer was gone; I knew that was so; and in its place, nesting and nestling within me in the darkness was a great tumor of sin, mirror-memory, and obligation.

I had a sudden and terrible sense of foreboding, of *déjà-vu*.

* * * * * * *

I made my way out of the bedroom and into the hallway. I remembered the way to Mengele's office... down a flight of stairs, across an eternity of thick gray-black carpet, a faint smell of antiseptic in the air. The door to Mengele's room was still ajar, and I walked in. Everything was as I had dreamed it earlier...as I had experienced it earlier, and my heart was a metronome beating fast in my throat, beating out the rhythm of my blood; and I approached Mengele's desk. I knew every object in the room, every book in the mahogany bookcases, the history and provenance of every curiosity, statue, and treasure.

And I knew Mengele.

I closed my eyes tight, then opened them again, hoping to change what was before me: Mengele was sprawled over his desk, his nose and face broken, his forehead resting on the leather framed blotter, which was stained and sticky with blood. The back of his head was shattered; the smell of blood was crisp and fresh and acrid.

I had killed him, and he had accepted the bullets.

No amount of closing my eyes would change anything.

"So it is done. You have both decided."

I jumped at the sound.

Gata stood in the doorway, incongruously dressed as in western clothes: tan trousers, white shirt, and a blue jacket. His heavy featured face was still divided into old and young, but the aged half was softer somehow, less withered.

"When did you find him?" I asked.

"As you did."

"Just now, this minute?"

He made the hnrung sound, sighed, and nodded.

I leaned across the desk and gingerly, gently touched Mengele's hand, which was cold. "But did you know what happened before...now?" I asked Gata, who looked hard at me.

"I saw what you might do, Meester; but the *Doutor*, only he knew what *he* would do. He told me a little, though...."

"What?" I asked.

"That if you both did this"—he gestured toward Mengele—"then *you* would become the *Doutor.*"

"I am no doctor."

"Ah, but you know how now, don't you, Meester? Now you can remember. He said it would all come to you. All his memories."

"And what else did he tell you?" I asked.

"That I was to help you, and then I would be free to go."

"And me?"

He shrugged. "You can go now."

"But not be free."

Gata laughed, something I had not heard him do before. It was a shrill, almost girlish sound. "You have him now, Meester, just as he had you before. You can do what you will; you are the *Doutor* now. Now if you will be pleased to go back to your room and rest, I will take care of this" He gestured at Mengele. "Then I will introduce you to the other doctors and nurses and *brujos* in the clinic."

"Is there a minister on the premises who can conduct a proper service?"

Another girlish laugh: Gata seemed quite light-hearted about the death of his master. "No, it is not necessary," he said, making a quick, fluttering gesture with his hand—a gesture used in the camps: the sign of smoke rising from the crematoria.

I took a sharp breath, remembering.

"The *Doutor* left instructions what was to be done. We have the facilities."

And as I turned to leave, Gata said, "There is one other thing the *Doutor* left for you, Meester," and he gave me a book.

Fiat Lux.

Mengele's diary.

* * * * * * *

I took the book back to my room and wrote an entry in the diary, and then I slept. Weighted down with memory, I dreamed of Onca, fat, bountiful, natural Onca. I dreamed of her heavy legs and thighs, her large earth mother breasts. I dreamed of the glassy manioc gruel and ice cream she made for me, which numbed me, chilled me like ether until all pain was distant... cold and distant as Mengele's memories.

And then my dreams spoke to hers.

"Onca...."

"Do not worry, Meester. You will help people until you are okay."

"Onca...."

"Have you got old yet?"

"I...."

"I can see you, Meester. You will be old, but all the way, not half one half other. Now you are a *claro sonhador*. Now you will live your dream right to the end."

"Onca...."

"Thank you for giving me my Genaro back... *Doutor*."

"You're welcome," I whispered as I slept and dreamed Mengele dreams.

ABOUT THE AUTHOR

JACK DANN is a multiple award-winning author who has written or edited over seventy-five books, including the groundbreaking novels *Junction, Starhiker, The Man Who Melted, The Memory Cathedral*—which was an international bestseller—the Civil War novel *The Silent*, and *Bad Medicine*, which has been compared to the works of Jack Kerouac and Hunter S. Thompson, and called "the best road novel since the *Easy Rider* days."

Dann's work has been compared to Jorge Luis Borges, Roald Dahl, Lewis Carroll, Castaneda, Ray Bradbury, J. G. Ballard, Mark Twain, and Philip K. Dick. Dick, the author of the stories from which the films *Blade Runner* and *Total Recall* were made, wrote that "*Junction* is where Ursula K. Le Guin's *The Lathe of Heaven* and Tony Boucher's 'The Quest for Saint Aquin' meet...and yet it's an entirely new novel.... I may very well be basing some of my future work on *Junction*." Best selling author Marion Zimmer Bradley called *Starhiker* "a superb book...it will not give up all its delights, all its perfections, on one reading."

Library Journal has called Dann "...a true poet who

can create pictures with a few perfect words." Roger Zelazny thought he was a reality magician, and *Best Sellers* has said that "Jack Dann is a mind-warlock whose magicks will confound, disorient, shock, and delight." *The Washington Post Book World* compared his novel *The Man Who Melted* with Ingmar Bergman's film *The Seventh Seal.*

His books have been widely translated, and his short stories have appeared in *Playboy, Omni, Penthouse, Asimov's*, "*Best of*" collections in Australia, the United States, and Great Britain, and other major magazines and anthologies. He is the editor of the anthology *Wandering Stars*, one of the most acclaimed American anthologies of the 1970s, and several other well-known anthologies such as *More Wandering Stars. Wandering Stars* and *More Wandering Stars* have recently been reprinted in the U.S. Dann also edited the multi-volume *Magic Tales* series with Gardner Dozois and is a consulting editor for Tor Books.

He is a recipient of the Nebula Award, the Australian Aurealis Award (twice), the Ditmar Award (four times), the World Fantasy Award, the Peter McNamara Achievement Award, the Peter McNamara Convenors Award for Excellence, and the *Premios Gilgamés de Narrativa Fantástica* award. Dann has also been honored by the Mark Twain Society (Esteemed Knight).

High Steel, a novel co-authored with Jack C. Haldeman II, was published in 1993 by Tor Books. Critic John Clute called it "a predator...a cat with blazing eyes gorging on the good meat of genre. It is most highly recommended." Dann is currently writing *Ghost Dance*, the sequel to *High Steel*, with Jack Haldeman's widow, author Barbara Delaplace.

Dann's major historical novel about Leonardo da Vinci—entitled *The Memory Cathedral*—was published to rave reviews. It has been published in over ten languages to date. It won the Australian Aurealis Award, was #1 on *The Age* bestseller list, and a story based on the novel was awarded the Nebula Award. *The Memory Cathedral* was also shortlisted for the Audio Book of the Year, which was part of the Braille & Talking Book Library Awards.

Morgan Llewelyn called *The Memory Cathedral* "a book to cherish, a validation of the novelist's art and fully worthy of its extraordinary subject." *The San Francisco Chronicle* called it "A grand accomplishment," *Kirkus Reviews* thought it was "An impressive accomplishment," and *True Review* said, "Read this important novel, be challenged by it; you literally haven't seen anything like it."

Dann's novel about the American Civil War, *The Silent*, was chosen as one of *Library Journal's* 'Hot Picks'. *Library Journal* wrote: "This is narrative storytelling at its best—so highly charged emotionally as to constitute a kind of poetry from hell. Most emphatically recommended." Peter Straub said "This tale of America's greatest trauma is full of mystery, wonder, and the kind of narrative inventiveness that makes other novelists want to hide under the bed." And *The Australian* called it "an extraordinary achievement."

His novel *Bad Medicine* (titled *Counting Coup* in the U.S.), a contemporary road novel, has been described by *The Courier Mail* as "perhaps the best road novel since the Easy Rider Days."

Dann is also the co-editor (with Janeen Webb) of the groundbreaking Australian anthology, *Dreaming Down-Under*, which Peter Goldsworthy called "the biggest, boldest, and most controversial collection of original fiction ever published in Australia." It won Australia's Ditmar Award and was the first Australian book ever to win the World Fantasy Award. His anthology, *Gathering the Bones*, of which he is a co-editor, was included in *Library Journal*'s Best Genre Fiction of 2003, and was shortlisted for The World Fantasy Award. His anthology, *Wizards*, co-edited with Gardner Dozois, and titled *Dark Alchemy* in the UK and Australia, made the Waldenbooks/Borders bestseller list, and was shortlisted for the World Fantasy Award. He has also edited a sequel to *Dreaming Down-Under*: *Dreaming Again*. The influential *Bookseller+Publisher* gave *Dreaming Again* a five star rating and wrote: "Here are stories that engage with the building blocks of our culture and others that give shape to our shared darkness and light. *Dreaming Again* is at once quintessentially Australian and enticingly other. If you read short fiction you'll want this collection. If you don't, this is a reason to start."

His most recent anthologies are *Dreaming Again*, *The Dragon Book* (with Gardner Dozois), *Australian Legends* (with Jonathan Strahan), and *Ghosts by*

Gaslight (with Nick Gevers).

Dann's stories have been collected in *Timetipping, Visitations,* and the retrospective short story collection *Jubilee: the Essential Jack Dann.* The *West Australian* said it was "Sometimes frightening, sometimes funny, erudite, inventive, beautifully written and always intriguing. *Jubilee* is a celebration of the talent of a remarkable storyteller." His collaborative stories can be found in his collection *The Fiction Factory.*

The *West Australian* called Dann's recent novel, *The Rebel: An Imagined Life of James Dean,* "an amazingly evocative and utterly convincing picture of the era, down to details of the smells and sensations—and even more importantly, the way of thinking." *Locus* wrote: "*The Rebel* is a significant and very gripping novel, a welcome addition to Jack Dann's growing oeuvre of speculative historical novels, sustaining further his long-standing contemplation of the modalities of myth and memory. This is alternate history with passion and difference." A companion James Dean short story collection entitled *Promised Land* has also been published in Great Britain, as has Dann's most recent short novel, *The Economy of Light.*

As part of its *Bibliographies of Modern Authors Series,* The Borgo Press has published an annotated bibliography and guide entitled *The Work of Jack Dann.* An updated second edition is in progress. Dann is also listed in *Contemporary Authors* and the *Contemporary Authors Autobiography Series; The International Authors and Writers Who's Who;*

Personalities of America; Men of Achievement; Who's Who in Writers, Editors, and Poets, United States and Canada; Dictionary of International Biography; the *Directory of Distinguished Americans; Outstanding Writers of the 20th Century;* and *Who's Who in the World*. His recently published autobiography is entitled *Insinuations*.

Dann lives in Australia on a farm overlooking the sea, and 'commutes' back and forth to Los Angeles and New York. He is married to the writer Janeen Webb.

His website is jackdann.com. You can also follow him on Twitter @jackmdann

JUBILEE

Peter Lindsay lives in Melbourne, Australia. Charles Blackford is an American trying to relive a happier time in Athens. Both men have lost their wives. And now they must decide how to cope with the overwhelming changes being wrought by transcendent emergences from the sea.

Library Journal called *Jubilee* "a haunting story of transformation and loss," and *The New York Review of Science Fiction* wrote that it is "a complex fantasy that reads like a collaboration between Lawrence Durrell and H. P. Lovecraft. How's that for literary ambition?"

Jubilee is *the* quintessential "First Contact" story, a mind-bendingly brilliant exploration into what is alien...and what it means to be human.

Borgo Press Books by JACK DANN

Da Vinci Rising
The Diamond Pit: A Science Fiction Novel
The Economy of Light
Jubilee

JUBILEE

JACK DANN

THE BORGO PRESS

MMXII

JUBILEE

DEDICATION

This book's for my comrade-in-arms,

Steve Paulsen

CONTENTS

The coming of the jubilee is usually sensed by one or another of a few people who have the gift of seeing the signs in the sea and air. When the signs appear, they go down to the shore and wait. If the feeling has been authentic, flounders and crabs begin to gather in holes in ankle-deep bottom, and eels soon turn up where no eels were before. When the eels come, word quickly spreads inland, and people begin to move down to the beach....
—Archie Carr, "A Celebration of Eden"

I found myself in a dilapidated hotel in Athens' ancient Turkish quarter where prices were inflated, the gawking German and American tourists were fleeced without even an obligatory smile, and the air was so polluted that I was already sniffing and coughing as if I had a cold.

I had been here before with Sandra, who loved this converted ninteenth-century mansion. She loved Athens, loved its noise and food and antiquity, and imagined she could see the ghosts of ancient Greeks like Socrates and Pericles walking the streets as we

ate squid and yogurt and oily *pastitsio* in an outdoor restaurant that overlooked the ruins of a Neolithic necropolis.

Now I was back. I had even requested our old room. But the room was all I had, for now I had no business, no home, no life. My books were in numbered boxes that lined the walls of a storage shed in upstate New York, as if mutely guarding the few pieces of furniture, prints, and cherished objects that I had taken from my old house.

And Sandra was now with someone else....

I unpacked my flight bag, took a shower, and then went out on my little balcony to look at the Saturday night tourists teeming below. The balcony was filthy, layered with dirt, and I wouldn't sit down on the white, sticky plastic chairs; below, the narrow back streets were littered with garbage. I could hear the background hum of the city, sense its jittery buzz, as if Greece was a nervous sleeper and Athens its choking, yearning, flash-flickering dream.

How I hated this garbage-strewn place; and yet here I was, drawn back, as if I could find solace in happy memories, in the twisting, vendor-infested streets; in the tavernas and hotels, or away in the hill country of factories and olive groves, and the cruel upthrusted islands overwhelmed by the sea.

But instead of happy memories, bad thoughts invaded my mind.

I could not help but think of Sandra with her new lover in our bed, and I knew that I had to get out of

my room, into open streets, into crowds. I had to keep moving. The plane ride from New York to LA and then to Paris and finally Athens had been its own hell. I could not bear to be alone, yet here I was in this ancient, alien place where I knew only the hotel manager, Aristides, who liked to get drunk with the European and American guests and then make surreptitious passes at their wives.

I smiled as I passed him at the bottom of the stairs.

"*Kalispera*, Mister Blackford," he said, promising to stay past his shift if I would only have an Ouzo with him.

"Perhaps later," I replied, and he grinned, as if he knew everything, as perhaps he did, for he did not ask about Sandra. But just as I was about to step into the hot, crowded street, I turned on impulse and walked back to his little desk. I needed something—or someone— to distract me from the past.

"Ari," I said in a low voice, "could you find me a woman?"

The manager gave me a sly, condescending look, as if he had forgotten himself, and then said, "This cannot be done, Mister Blackford, not here, this is not that kind of hotel. Did you not see me have to kick that poor woman out of the bar earlier. She wanted a room for two thousand Drachmas."

An English family came down the stairs, everyone saying hello to Ari, who smiled at them benevolently and waved to the children.

I felt my face become hot, for surely they had heard

Ari talking.

"But you have been a good friend to me," he said before they were even through the doorway. "You have drank into the night with me. " Then, in a low, conspiratorial voice, he said, "I will do what I can to help you. I know someone who might know someone. But it will be expensive...."

Suddenly I just wanted to get out of this narrow, dirty, paneled lobby. It was difficult to breathe. The heat and the steamy walls were pressing in on me. I had humiliated myself, and the very idea of being with a woman gave me claustrophobia.

But what was I afraid of?

Being hurt again?

And then I realised that I felt guilty, as if *I* was cheating on Sandra.

But *she* had cheated on me.

"Perhaps 50,000 Drachmas."

I turned toward the glass doors, as if Ari's whisper was a shout, exposing me. I was too embarrassed to look at him directly, but as I left, I saw his reflection in the dark, smeary glass: his merry, pudgy face and thin moustache. He looked as satisfied as a cat that had drawn blood.

And as I walked down Nikis Avenue, pushing past the tourists looking for dinner or looking in shop windows at reproductions of ancient vases and plates and pots and statues, or looking at fake icons slathered with silver and gold, I noticed that something was amiss: the streets were quiet.

Oh, the tourists were chattering and scuffing and pointing, but the shop owners weren't standing outside their stores, selling their wares; and the maître d's weren't pushing and corralling the Americans and Germans and Japanese into their courtyards.

What was going on? It wasn't a religious holiday.

As I wandered through the bricked, narrow streets of the Plaka—the Acropolis a well-lit, floating mirage on the hill above—I realised how alien this place felt without Sandra. It was like being in a familiar wood on a summer night and wondering why the cicadas were quiet.

And as I edged out of the tourist area, out of the center of the ancient Plaka, Athens became dead quiet.

Which was...impossible.

* * * * * * *

After his wife Nedra died, Peter Lindsay began to dream of water deep and green and bright, as if lit from its depths by klieg lights as bright as the noon sun. He had the same dream every night. He did not dream of Nedra, bless her sweet, gentle soul; he did not dream of his past, of his youth, or of missed opportunities; but just as Hemingway's old man dreamed every night of his lions, so did Peter Lindsay dream of the ocean. An ocean that was as alive as the lions, that breathed and sighed and whispered, whispered the answers to all the questions.

The ocean contained all the creatures.

All the creatures that had come vast distances to

dream the world anew....

Although several months passed before Peter realised it, he had stopped painting. He still awakened at dawn, made coffee, played loud jazz on his ancient stereo, and spent the hours in the studio behind his dilapidated house, working in oils or water colours; but he worked a little less every day, and slept a little more, until he could smell the tang of the ocean, feel it buoying him, carrying him away from the lurching, frantic darkness of sleep into emerald light. Pulling him.

When he was awake, he felt tired. Drugged.

When he slept, he heard voices like static mixed with the rushing of the sea. And as he grew weaker, dying a little more as he drifted further away, he began to differentiate voices. The sea was sound and speech.

It was white and sharp as pain.

Hospital white.

There he could finally fall back into grief, into life, which was green, glaucous green, and as large and bright and purple shadowed as the creeping, encroaching rain forest. But that was just another dream, like that of the ocean, as large as the ocean: a sea of living foliated green....

* * * * * * *

I didn't venture out of the Plaka, nor did I stop in any of the tavernas or ouzeria. They certainly weren't empty, for I passed a courtyard full of German tourists, who seemed to be having a grand time eating and drinking; and indeed the tourists seemed somehow

more real than anything or anyone else around me. Perhaps it was an effect of the light, for they seemed like characters on a stage, clear and defined, while everything else was drowned in shadow.

As I left the German tourists behind, the streets became muffled once again.

I said hello to a passerby, just to hear the sharpness of a voice, even if my own; and I anticipated the delicious, plosive retort of "*kalispera*." But there was no response, for I was as shadowy and evanescent as the grey haired fellow who walked silently by me.

When I passed the ruins of the Agora, which had once been the hub of ancient Athens, I realised that I had gotten turned around. All the narrow, winding, crisscrossing streets in the old quarter looked alike. I was surprised to find hundreds of people pressing against a high mesh fence that enclosed the ruins of the Agora, which were barely illuminated by surrounding street lamps. Yet the crowd was unnaturally quiet. It was made up mostly of women dressed in traditional black with shawls pulled over their heads; the men were kneeling.

They were all praying.

I had, of course, been here before; it was a tourist attraction, a great, fenced-in archaeological garbage heap, with piles of stone scattered everywhere. Here was where Socrates lectured any citizen who would listen, here was where Saint Paul proselytised for a new millennium.

What could these people be looking at?

What could they be praying to?

I made my way to the chain-link fence and shouldered my way between two women, who were fingering their rosaries and praying as if their very lives depended on every word and motion. And I realised that I could hear a thousand beads clicking around me, as if a thousand roulette wheels were spinning.

I stared hard into the Agora.

All the ancient stones were still there—the alters and stoa and piles tagged for restoration—but what had been sandy ground was now covered with a gnarly carpet of grass and vine, its thick tangle was everywhere, and in the dim light it looked so dark as to be purple. Vines were curled around the piles of cut stones, connecting them like sail shrouds, and directly before me, the vines and shoots and what looked like the trunks and limbs of olive trees had taken a definite architectural shape: three columns separated by arches. And in the arches were masses that looked like bells.

A church made of trunk and vine.

* * * * * * *

Peter Lindsay was back home. Had he been gone a day, a week...a month? He still felt disoriented, as if he had just awakened in the wrong house; but indeed this was his house, the familiar one story 1890's Victorian gingerbread nestled between the million dollar duplexes that had just been built within the last year. He stared out his kitchen window that overlooked the street as if

he were alone, while his friend Stephen, who had just brought him home from the hospital, was puttering by the sink, making tea.

How could Nedra be dead? Peter asked himself. It seemed a cruel trick, for nothing else had changed: the neighbour's yard across the street was afire with red and gold flowers; their white cement house, which was as old as his own, reminded him of a mosque; and he thought that he might have been in Tunisia or Morocco instead of Melbourne, Australia. His little street was quiet, but for the occasional car. If he listened, though, he could hear the heavy traffic on Punt Road, the street behind the house, a reminder that he lived near the center of a city of three million people. He had lost part of his back yard ten years ago when they widened Punt Road to turn it into an avenue, and he had gotten used to the constant background noise: the dull roar of engines, the plashing of tires, and the sudden horns and sirens. He had learned to paint to the new rhythm of traffic; he thought of it as the rushing of blood in his arteries. Not even double glazed windows could keep it out.

But now, as he looked at quiet Affleck Street, with its new extrusions of townhouses, he *felt* Nedra's absence. And every knickknack on the windowsill, every lithograph and woodcut on the kitchen wall, even the old stains on the floor seemed...haunted. The room grew thick with the ghosts of the past; and Peter remembered, remembered living in Ithaca, New York, remembered meeting Nedra at an outdoor art show in

Atlantic City where he was exhibiting his paintings and graphics. She was tall and blond and freckled and sunburnt, and she had long fingers and chewed half-moon fingernails. She had bought Peter's woodcut of a fern, a miniature, and he followed her here, to her house, 9,000 miles away from home.

That was twenty years ago.

Peter gazed at the woodcut of the fern on the kitchen wall; Nedra had insisted on hanging it in the kitchen because that was the heart of the house. He stood up and removed it from the wall. But the smooth frame slipped out of his hands, and glass and wood broke on the hardwood floor.

"I'll clean up the glass," Stephen said, gently leading Peter back to the kitchen table and a cup of tea. Stephen was in his early fifties, an accountant with a black beard, high forehead, and frizzy greying hair tied into a ponytail. He was dressed in jeans and a faded work-shirt, the same clothes he would wear to his office.

"Leave it," Peter said. "I'll get it later. What you can do is take me for a drive."

Stephen looked surprised. "If you need groceries, I can pick them up while you settle back in."

Peter pulled on his beard—an old habit as obsessive as children twisting their hair when daydreaming. Nedra called it "woolgathering." His beard was white and long and considerably thicker than his hair. "I want to go out to the rain forest." He forced a grin. "The trams won't take me that far."

"You haven't even unpacked your bags. How about I

take you tomorrow?"

"You've already taken time off today."

"To get you settled in," Stephen said.

"And I appreciate that, and all the other trouble you've gone to for me."

"It was no trouble," Stephen said emphatically. "I told you, I'm happy to be able to pay back a little for all the time and help and good advice you've given me over the years."

"Well, then take me for a drive."

"Peter, you just got out of the hospital."

"And I'm damned well fucking determined not to go back. So humor me. I miss Nedra so much that I can't catch my breath. I miss her especially now that I'm back...home. But I'm not going to curl into a ball; I'm going to paint like never before. That's what she would have wanted. I'm going to paint for her. You just fucking watch me."

"Well, you're certainly sounding like your old self."

"Come on, we'll do male-bonding, and I'll tell you what it was like in the loony bin." Peter was fond of Stephen, who had been buying his paintings for years. Stephen used to say that he had the money, but Peter had the answers. Peter had made good friends in this country; they had all given him what support they could. But Nedra had always been the strong one. Hadn't she consoled him while she fought the cancer that was metastasizing into her kidneys, liver, and lung? Hadn't she finally kicked him and the nurses out of her room so she could get on with the business of

dying? "It's a job I've got to do by myself," she had told him.

"You weren't in the loony bin," Stephen insisted. "You were in the respiratory wing because your lung collapsed. You were exhausted, and after what you went through, who wouldn't be?" After a beat, he asked, "Don't you remember?"

"Yes, of course I remember," Peter said. "Now take me for a ride in your expensive Jaguar."

"Why the rain forest?"

"Because I want to paint it. I need to refresh my eyes; I haven't been in the bush for years."

He didn't tell Stephen that he had dreamed of the rain forest after his operation, when he was coming out of the anaesthesia. He had also dreamed of the ocean, dreamed of alien beings swimming and gliding in the deep wastes.

Huge floating creatures that were themselves dreaming....

* * * * * * *

Are you the creature dreaming, as the reef spawns, as the coral discharges its egg and sperm into the watery light of the full moon? The sea is black glass, its calm surface hiding the hot agitation in its depths. Gill-dreams of new life, ancient life, breaking the surface, changing everything; as you wait in the rolling darkness.

Are you the sea or the creature? The alien or the indigene? The answer or the conundrum?

Are you the messiah at the end of time turned serene nightmare or just a great seawall of star spotted dorsal skin, a highway of lateral ridges and electromagnetic sensory pores? Are you the beast at the end of the world? Even now the sea changes, and reefs grow not by slow accretion but in whole stands. Sea change in the crystal waters of the South Pacific, in the once dead, fished-out Mediterranean now pregnant with skate and shark and ray, now aglow in red and yellow profusions of coral.

From without or within—from the stars or the watery bowels of the earth—do you dream as the great Parisian avenues of Melbourne become canals for gondoliers and Athens turns into Atlantis?

* * * * * * *

"*Pos i-ste*, Mister Blackford?" Ari asked as I stepped into the lobby, which was empty, as was the adjoining combination bar and breakfast room.

"I'm very well, thank you," I said, impatient to get back to my room; but I had to tell Ari to cancel the whore. Being with a stranger would only intensify my sense of loss. I just needed some sleep...just some sleep. "Ari—"

"No, no, Mister Blackford, it's all taken care of." Ari flung his hands up, and I stepped back reflexively. He laughed at that. "And everything has been done with great discretion."

"That's what I wanted to talk to you about. I've changed my mind."

"No, it's too late. It's all settled."

"Ari, I'll take care of any embarrassment this might cause you. How much to take care of it?"

He would not look at me directly and stared into his guest record book. "I will not see this person again tonight."

"Doesn't he have a phone?"

He shrugged. "It's not possible."

"All right, Ari. Goodnight."

But as I turned to leave he said, "I will tell the girl when she comes...if I am here. If it's too late, then—" He shrugged.

"Thanks, I'd appreciate that very much."

Perhaps my voice was surly and he thought he'd surely lose his tip of 5,000 drachmas at the end of my stay, for he asked, "Would you like some Ouzo? It's on the house."

"Not tonight, Ari, perhaps tomorrow." But before I left him, I asked, "Is today some sort of religious holiday?"

"No, I don't think so. It may be some minor fast day, that I wouldn't know." He grinned at me, as if we were both involved in a conspiracy against the Greek Orthodox Church. Yet he wore a silver crucifix and a saint's medallion around his neck...just in case. "Did you find people going to church?"

"No, but I walked down to the Agora—"

"Aha...."

"What's going on there?" I asked.

"Did you look in?"

"Yes," I said, somehow feeling defensive.

"And what did you see when you looked in?" He suddenly looked quite interested.

"It was too dark to make anything out," I said, lying.

He nodded, as if confirming something to himself.

"Well?" I asked.

"It's a miracle. That's what I've been told. But only for us."

"What do you mean?"

"For Christians."

"How do you know *I'm* not a Christian?"

"Because I know you are Jewish." He smiled, but seemed distracted.

"Tell me about this miracle at the Agora?" I asked, probing, but he only shrugged. "Have you been there?"

"I think I will go tonight."

"You must have heard *something* about it," I insisted.

"It's a miracle, that's all I know."

"I didn't see anything about it on the English language channel. Is there anything in the papers?"

Ari shrugged. "It would not be in them or on the television."

"Why not?"

"Because it is a real miracle." He nodded again and said, "I will go tonight."

"Is that why the streets are so quiet?" I was humoring him, yet even as I said it, I realised I wanted to know the answer.

"I will go tonight," Ari said, ignoring my question; and as I climbed the stairs to my room, I could hear

the faint clicking and clacking of his worry beads as he dropped the amber stones, one atop the other, down to the knot at the end of their silver thread.

Or perhaps it was a rosary.

* * * * * * *

They drove with the top down because it was after 3:00 PM and the UV radiation was in the safe zone, or so said the radio announcer on the FOX station. Peter enjoyed the warm flat feel of sunlight on his face and the wind whipping his long white hair about, enjoyed the hot smell of February's summer, and the clear sharp air that was so transparent he could see the veins in leaves fifty feet away. This was certainly not Italy, or New York State with its heavy, water vapour atmosphere that blunted the edges of things, that veiled the world. Here was clarity; and Peter inhaled it all as if he had just been given a reprieve from death. This was Nedra's gift to him, even as the poignancy of her loss clotted like thick phlegm in the back of his throat.

He would stay in the moment. For this moment and the next he would not think of what had been lost: he felt twenty-five, and he was going to paint his ass off; he was going to find the colours that were in the inside of things, not just what could be only seen with the eyes. Synaesthesia. He had felt the colours before, when he had first started painting, when he had been so swept up in the very act of putting brush and colour to canvas that he forgot all analytical skill. Then he could hear a music that was like a differentiated thunder:

musical tones of the rainbow. He closed his eyes and imagined that he was flying, flying just feet away from the macadam in Stephen's waxed leather and wood scented XJ40 Daimler Jaguar, swept into a bright cone of greenness ahead; and he could see the colours shifting as if in a kaleidoscope, each shade melding into another like emotion itself: absinth, green apple, aquamarine, beryl, bice, and bottle green; chrysoidine and chrysolite and chrysoprase, corbeau and cobalt green, green exploding, evaporating, melting like metal into milori and mitis and moss, into peas and patina and terre-verte, into serpentine and shamrock and sea-water fronds reaching toward him, cool and wet and undulating jade, a rainforest of green, choking, inhaling, fertilising everything, overwhelming everything that was.

And Peter came awake with a jolt and looked around. They had driven out of Central Melbourne on the Maroondah Highway and were now in the northern suburbs, the Dandenongs. Green dreams had dissolved into miles of grey strip malls: chockablock MacDonalds, Coles, Hungry Jacks; carparks, department stores, computer stores; industrial parks and auction barns. This could easily be Hempstead, Long Island or Paramus, New Jersey. But Stephen was heavy footed, and they roared down the highway at around 140 kilometres an hour; other cars seemed to be standing still. Soon they were in the Upper Yarra Valley, driving past grey-barked gum trees and sheep and cattle grazing in dull yellow fields, and through

the bush, a thick canopy of trees shading the road. In the distance were ancient mountains, blue-tinged from air heavy with eucalyptus. Nearer were yellowish hills; small copses of trees stood upon their swells like toy soldiers. Farm country. Bush. Miles without sight of habitation. Green and gold country. God's country.

The road narrowed, turned from two laned macadam to dirt. Stephen turned off the road. A sign nailed to a tree read TALL TREES, and Stephen parked the green Jag, now grey with dust, on the shoulder. This was temperate rain forest, cool and autumnal; the narrow-boled gum trees rose into the grey light above, and giant ferns shivered in the woody air like shields held by warriors waiting to march into battle.

Peter had not told Stephen of his dreams, or how it had been in the hospital; in fact, neither man had spoken very much during the trip. Each seemed to be isolated, and Peter was certain that Stephen wished himself anywhere else but here in this green and brown nowhere of mountain ash so tall that one had to bend backwards to see their tops. Yet Peter didn't care. That thought itself jolted him. Well, he'd make it up to Stephen. He would give him a painting, or perhaps one of the pastels he intended on working on here.

Stephen followed him along the worn path into the forest; they had not gone more than a few hundred feet when they encountered fallen trees and brush over the path. Looking for the right place to sketch, Peter pushed through on his own.

"Is it going to bother you, me hanging around while

you paint?" Stephen asked. "I could just as well go back to the car."

"It won't bother me at all," Peter said. "I'll just make some quick sketches, and then we can get out of here." But why would anyone want to leave this place? he asked himself. This was bliss. The place seemed to have a depth of colour and space Peter couldn't find in the city; and he started working, his hand moving as if of its own volition, sketching in rough outlines, then the soft, dry smearing of pastel, the cool chalky feel of it on the fingers, clean and sure; and he gazed into the distance, as if the forest were his sketchbook, and he sensed the luminous order of this place in the trees that appeared like the columns of some natural heliotropic temple. But his reverie was broken when Stephen said he was going back to the car.

"What time is it?" Peter asked.

"Well, old son, you've been painting for over two hours." Stephen smiled, as if he was pleased. "I'm going to take a whiz and sit in the air con. It's gotten fucking humid out here. Take your time. My shrink will be more than pleased that I've been forced to just hang out and enjoy nature...and take a piss in the forest."

"Okay, I'm done," Peter said, lying. "Give me a minute, and I'll have all this stuff put away."

"No you *won't*," Stephen insisted. "Do I really have to have company when I pee? Take your time. I really am enjoying it out here. But all this fresh air makes me feel sleepy." Then he gazed out into the forest as

if Peter wasn't there. It was as if he was transfixed, or was somehow dreaming with his eyes open.

"Steve, are you okay?" Peter asked.

"I was just thinking about something. I'll see you in a while." And with that he walked away.

"Steve, what were you thinking about?"

Stephen stopped, turned around, and looked past his friend. He blinked, as if he were looking into the sun. "The trees were just playing tricks on my eyes."

"What kind of tricks?"

But Stephen disappeared, leaving Peter to look into the forest, where Stephen had been staring.

The light changed, as if clouds had passed across the sun. The trees and ferns seemed to form an arbor... no, not an arbor, that wasn't it. The trunks and limbs of the trees had taken a definite architectural shape: three columns separated by arches. And in the arches were masses that looked like bells. A church.

Peter looked away, relaxing his eyes, then stared again. But the illusion wouldn't be shaken.

He set his pastel kit and sketchbook on the ground and walked toward the phantom church, looking away from it, then into it, as if to shake away its substance; but the illusion of bells and arches was broken only when he was almost upon the spot. He looked past what had been woody arches and stepping through them, felt warmth. It was as if the atmosphere had suddenly changed, becoming hot and humid. Even the odours were different: pungent, overpowering, as if everything was ripe and rotting, both flesh and vege-

table. And as the light shifted, this new place became tangible, palpable, and he knew what had happened. He, or this place, had slipped backwards, the past was somehow intermingling with the present, hot with cold, temperate with tropical. The forest was here, too, but this was the lush forest of tropical Queensland a thousand miles to the north. It was so thick that the sun could barely shine through its roof of leaf and branch and grasping fern. The trees were straight-stemmed, narrow boled, and encrusted with lichens and clusters of brilliant flowers and fruits. The hues and complexities were those of a Breughel painting, dark and deep and mysterious. Peter could smell the damp greenness. The pointed drip-tip leaves were huge, as were the ferns that seemed to be caught in some millennium-long motion, in mid-stride across the world; and lianas and epiphytes hung from the high tree limbs, twisted and tangled around branch and stem, winding along the forest floor like snakes, connecting the canopy, pulling the steaming, hot barked fingers into a great fist, growing, growing.

Peter was drenched with sweat.

Turn around, get out of here, he told himself, swallowing hard, as if panic could be dissolved in saliva. But where had he come in? There were no arches, no church, no path back to the safety of the familiar. He whispered to himself, a nonsensical droning, a barely audible pleading; and he was electrified with fear, for he imagined that this place was made of up eyes, eyes watching him from every direction, every angle; and

then he talked out loud to himself, as he might to a frightened child, that this was a dream, that there was nothing to be afraid of.

But this was not the dream. The dream had been....

Of rainforest, yes, here, this.

But it was ocean, the recurring dream had been of ocean and the great dreaming creatures that would dwarf ships yet resembled them, ships of flesh, with pores for eyes...eyes that had seen distant worlds, Dresden blue eyes watching, dreaming, and changing the very stuff of being.

He heard something move, something snap, but it was his own foot stepping upon dead branch and vine. He froze, as if some ancient, racial memory had taken over, the response of prey, trapped, to become the background, as if what is still cannot be seen. For he could feel the weight of distant vision, not the feral, hot-eyed, mammalian glare. And as he looked at the large leaves hanging before him, leaves tipped crimson and splotched with blue, blue the colour of ancient, alien eyes, he saw them, saw them watching him, as if he were looking into mirrors; and the eyes gazed at him from years and infinities away. Peter felt caught; and he could sense the presence of the creatures from his dreams, the smooth behemoths swimming in the black alien depths of the sea; creatures dreaming and swimming, one the same as the other, dreaming him, dreaming him inside green dreams of root and vine and frond, chlorophyll dreams swimming out of the blue; and he could sense their thoughts, or some part

of a vast machinery of thought, so large and so slow as to almost thicken into substance.

But he could not reach into their depths, only dream the surface: green sea turning blue. The ocean, mother mystery, pulling at him with green rainforest fingers, the world slipping back into dreamtime, pulling him back.

Leaf eyes staring, Peter crashed through them, running to hide, to escape, an aging Adam in a malevolent unblinking Eden.

Sick with fear, he fled in the direction he had come: back to the familiar. Yet even as he did, a distant voice, the tinny voice of his consciousness, said, "*You can't go back.*" Tubers caught at his feet, his legs. He pressed himself past the thin-bowled trees being strangled by parasite roots, past glistening ferns spotted with crimson and turquoise, as if all pigments had been dreamed into this green reality.

And then he was free.

He stopped, tried to catch his breath, and found himself standing on his pastels, crushing the cylindrical, colored pieces into the soft loamy dirt. The air was dry and cool. Only he was drenched and sweating. He looked for the arching church, and, indeed, when he began to calm down, he could see its natural columns and arches once again. They seemed so much closer in the softer light of the late afternoon.

* * * * * * *

Although it was a warm night, I closed the windows

and the balcony shutters. October was usually a cooler month, the last gasp of the tourist season, but the weather hadn't changed. Who knows, perhaps it wouldn't. Aristides had turned off the air conditioning on September 30 and wouldn't turn it on again if the temperature rose to 100 degrees. I didn't care. It was quiet, the world was shut out, I was safe. I thought of Sandra sleeping with her lover in our bed, but my face didn't get hot and my digestive juices didn't start eating my stomach.

Throughout the last few weeks, I had tried to locate the pain, that region of loss and loneliness, and discovered it was in the pit of my stomach. I felt as if I was constantly hungry, yet the thought of food made me queasy. Although I usually slept with my fist pressed against my chest, as if to prevent the aching and burning from expanding, tonight I lay on my back and stared at the stained ceiling.

I had been happy to move out of the house, to split all our assets, get an amicable divorce, and start life fresh. The children were grown and in college. They were old enough to understand, and I would support them and pay for their education. But the pain didn't start until I found out that Sandra had been having an affair.

For years. For fucking years.

Still, no reaction. No change in my breathing. No constriction. No claustrophobia. I reached for the fraying lamp cord that hung between the bed and night table and pushed the plastic switch. The room was so

dark as to appear flat. Perhaps tonight I would sleep. I hadn't slept more than five hours at a time for the last month.

If only I could stop thinking about Sandra, about the past, I could sleep. I thought of the sea, of warm, long curlers on a shelf of virgin white sand. I visualised a place where the sea and sky were one and the same, and realised it was Lefkada, an island where Sandra and I had been happy. But the whisper of the sea soothed me, spoke to me with distinct voices, caressed me, then turned into a roaring crashing pounding and

I woke up, gasping for breath.

Someone was knocking at the door.

I bumped my eyeglasses off the night table as I tried to find the light switch, and then I realised who it must be. No, I wouldn't turn on the light. I would wait until she left. But she was insistent. She would knock, then wait. I imagined I could hear her breathing outside the door, and I thought of swimming, of mermaids, of sea sounds, I remembered my dream of Lefkada; and feeling my way to the door, I let the whore in. For company, out of curiosity, I don't know. Perhaps it was loneliness. She had awakened me from a dream I wished wouldn't end, and I was...frightened now to be alone in the clammy darkness.

She was tiny, barely five feet tall, with very long, very thick black hair. She could have been Sandra, and for an instant I caught my breath; but in the dark, at midnight, any woman with a petite build and dark hair would have jagged my imagination. She closed the

door behind her, but said nothing, nor did she reach for me in the flat darkness.

As I was reluctant to turn on a light, I said, "*Si-gno-mi*," and felt my way across the room to the windows. I pulled open the shutters, letting in moonlight and city light, but when I looked down at the street, I saw dark water streaming and rippling between the old office buildings and apartment houses. It was as if the sea had broken through a great dam to fill the dusty, dirty streets of the city with clear fast-flowing water, white water sweeping silently as oil leaking over ancient cobblestones and steps. It wasn't water, of course, simply an effect of light and mist and humidity. Yet I couldn't help but feel that I was looking into reality, into someone else's dream of the future; and as I stood there looking into Athens' watery light, I felt the prostitute's arms slide around my naked waist, felt her flesh press against my back; in that instant, I found a relief from private pain. I felt a new security, a poignant longing for the ocean, for green islands and blue sea, for what might lie in its shimmering depths.

And as we made our clutching way back to the bed, as we tore at each other, as if ecstasy was a pain that could be only momentarily endured, I imagined I could hear the voices of the sea, as if I had lifted a conch shell to my ear.

The voices whispered, and in that instant of gasping pain I felt completely alone.

As if only I could swim.

* * * * * * *

Stephen had taken the Jag.

Perhaps he had gone for help. Perhaps he thought Peter was lost or hurt. Or, perhaps, he had followed Peter into the bush, into the rainforest, and panicked.

Peter waited two hours and then walked out to the main highway, which was choked with cars, as if this was a public holiday. He walked along the road's shoulder until he came to the source of the jam: a head-on collision between a Volvo and a small Russian made car. Glass had shattered across the road, and the bodies of the cars were twisted one into the other, like shiny, chitinous burrowing beasts. Slowly, cars were making their way around the accident, over the glass-strewn road shoulder. Peter crossed the road and peered inside the Volvo and the Russian car. Although the seats and smashed windshields were stained with blood, the cars were empty. The ambulance must have already come and gone, Peter thought. Surely wreckers would have towed away the cars, and road crews would have swept away the debris. But where were the police?

On either side of the road, the bush looked thicker and darker. Peter remembered walking through the scrim of one reality into another, from bush into deep, tropical rain forest; and although he *knew* it was real, it felt like a dream. Just as he knew that Nedra was dead, that she would not be waiting for him when he returned home. The bush—the thick knot of trees and climbers that deepened into green darkness, into a greener darkness than should have been ordinarily possible—seemed somehow impersonally malevolent.

Peter could feel the bush, the forest, the dreaming weight of it. He hurried, wanting only to escape it, for he imagined that it was staring hard at him, trying to possess him. Perhaps he should have stayed in the hospital.

Perhaps....

No!, and he stepped into the road, extending his thumb for a ride, forcing those drivers who would pass him to steer around him.

A woman driving a small, but very new and polished Japanese car picked him up. She was overweight, pretty with a ruddy, freckled complexion and brownish-red hair, which was heavily sprayed; and she looked to be in her late thirties. She seemed nervous. "I usually don't pick up hitchhikers." She brushed her fingers back and forth over the cellular phone handset cradled between the seats as if she was dusting it.

"Well, I haven't hitchhiked since I was a kid," Peter said, trying to calm her. "A friend gave me a ride out here and then left me stranded. I'm a bit worried about him. For a second, when I saw those cars wrapped around each other, I thought it might have been him. But, thank God, it wasn't." Peter waited for her to take the bait and talk about the accident.

"You have an American accent," she said, looking slightly less tense, as if being an American was credential enough.

"Well, I've lived here for twenty years." After a beat, Peter said, "My wife just died."

"I'm sorry," she said distractedly as she stopped and

waited to turn onto the macadam road. Traffic was heavy.

"Where are you from?" Peter asked.

She accelerated onto the highway; the little car certainly had zip. "Melbourne."

Peter waited for her to continue, but she drove on in silence, an uncomfortable silence. "I thought that accident back where you picked me up was very odd."

Still no response.

Peter shrugged and leaned away from her, against the window. He would not try to force conversation with her. It was enough that she had given him a ride. Why had she? he asked himself.

"Why do you think the accident was odd?" she asked. She seemed tense again. "An ambulance must have taken the people in the cars to hospital. They just haven't cleaned up yet."

"I would expect police to be directing traffic," Peter said, "and cordoning the area."

"Police are too busy."

"Doing what?"

She shrugged. "There have been a lot of drownings."

"Drownings?"

"I called my sister while I was tangled up in traffic, waiting for the accident to sort itself out. She lives in St. Kilda, a few blocks from the beach, and she told me that she had never seen so many police around there. Seems people have just been walking into the water and drowning."

"I'll bet it was a shark attack," Peter said. "We've

had problems before. And people panic and think they see all sorts of things." He felt a chill even as he said it. How could he tell anyone what *he* had seen? Somehow the drownings were connected with the creatures in his dreams...and with the forest that was—even now—watching them.

"No," she insisted. "My sister told me just what I told you."

"But that wouldn't affect the police out here." Peter said.

"Something's going on here, just like in St. Kilda. I tried calling the police emergency number, to make sure the accident back where I picked you up was properly reported and because traffic had completely stopped—and that wasn't exactly a four-lane freeway back there."

"What happened when you called?" Peter asked.

"I couldn't get through. The line was constantly engaged." She rubbed the corner of her mouth with her index finger, correcting her lipstick. Peter suspected it was a nervous habit.

"Did you try again?"

She handed the phone to Peter, who dialled 000.

The line was busy.

* * * * * *

When I woke up, it was still dark; yet I could see faint greyness through the balcony door windows. I sat up on the side of the bed, completely awake. Jet lag. There was a rustling behind me; and I found myself

looking at my reflection in black window glass, for the prostitute had turned on the lamp on the bed table. But I could not see her in the glass. Well, vampires have no reflection, I thought sourly. Yet I did not feel soiled. And as *she* had insisted on using a prophylactic, I thought my chances were quite good that I hadn't been infected.

"I'm sorry I woke you up," I said, not yet turning around. I really didn't know what she looked like: my only glimpse of her was in the dimly lit hallway and when she turned on the bathroom light, which was on the wall outside. For the first few breathless moments I had pretended that she was Sandra, and I felt the edges of a familiar emptiness; but she didn't feel or taste like Sandra, and I discovered that I didn't want Sandra; I just wanted to be blind in the sweat-scented darkness.

"You will tell me that I look like your wife, no?" she asked, coming around the bed to stand in front of me. I was shocked, I must admit, for there was a resemblance. But Sandra, always a girl-child, had become brittle and too polished; this woman would soften and fade with the years. I could see lines around her eyes; she was certainly in her late thirties, and her body was more voluptuous than Sandra's. She turned around and pulled her hair away from her neck. "Zip me up, please."

When I had pulled the loop of thread over a tiny hook that neatly closed the top of her dress, she turned around. "Well, do I look like her?"

"No," I said, easing away from her.

"Ari thought I did." She looked out the balcony into the grey light and smiled. "But many men think I look like women they love. I think there are many women with dark hair and faces like mine."

"How much do I owe you?"

"Whatever you agreed with Ari."

I gave her 50,000 Drachmas, which she counted. She smiled and said, "You did not cheat me. Good bye." With that she closed the door.

"Wait." I dashed to the door and opened it.

"Yes?"

"Where are you going?"

"To church."

"May I come with you?" I asked.

She studied me and said, "Yes, but only if you promise not to ask me stupid questions."

"Such as why you're going to church at dawn?"

"Or why such a nice girl would fuck you for money."

* * * * * * *

"Do you need to drive this fast?" Peter asked. They were in the suburbs, driving through the bright afternoon tunnel of strip malls and fast food chains; and Mary-Ellen—she had finally told him her name—was tailgating and weaving erratically through the traffic.

"I want to make sure my sister's all right."

"But you just talked to her."

"When I tried to call her again, she didn't answer the phone."

"Then what's the rush?" Peter asked. "We can try

her again now, and if she doesn't answer, we'll try her again later. She probably just stepped out."

Mary-Ellen rubbed the corner of her mouth.

"Why are you so anxious? Peter asked.

"Just a feeling."

"Feeling?" Peter became uncomfortable. He would have preferred small-talk, for he sensed she was going to draw him to her, entangle him. He thought of Stephen. Perhaps it was time to call him; he would certainly be home by now."

We're very close," Mary-Ellen said. "We're six years apart, but we always know when something's wrong. Would you come with me to check on her? I'll take you to your home right after."

Peter remembered a woman who had picked him up when he was hitch-hiking. That was forty years ago. Once the car was in motion, she had told him that she was afraid to drive alone because something had just gone wrong with the brakes.

"Well?" asked Mary-Ellen. "Will you go with me?"

Peter agreed, then asked to make a call. Stephen wasn't home; neither was Mary-Ellen's sister; and as she drove through Melbourne's streets, between the 1970's reflecting glass monoliths and past the turn of the century iron lacework façades and ever-present gardens, he told her what he had seen in the rainforest. He glanced at her as he talked, but her face was neutral, and he was unable to tell what she thought from her expression. Yet it was easier to talk to this stranger than it would have been to tell Stephen. He could have

told Nedra, may she rest in peace; surely he could have told her. She would have believed him.

Rest in peace....

So now he could admit that she was dead; her death was penetrating him slowly and deeply, like the bitter cold winter nights in Ithaca, New York. And as he talked, as he remembered what he had seen, as he visualised the rainforest, he imagined that he could look right into its arches, into its green darkness, as if he was looking into dark glass. The faint reflections were the stuff of dreams and thought, the diaphanous shapes of possibility. A thousand epiphanies, a thousand transformations.

* * * * * * *

We walked quickly along the dead labyrinthine streets, for she seemed to be in a hurry. When I asked, she told me that her name was Georgia; I didn't argue, or try to find out her real name. It was still dark, but there was a bit of grey in the sky, prefiguring dawn. All was shadow and emptiness. An occasional car sped by, dangerously fast, taking up most of the street; but the city was asleep; and all these narrow cobbled streets, the walls of windowed flats and storefronts, the paper devils and rusted cans—even the cars— seemed somehow insubstantial, dream projections of the millions of sleepers in the millions of apartments and houses and hotel rooms that formed a hive capped by the Acropolis, which was uncharacteristically dark. The klieg lights must have been turned off at the first

glimpse of morning.

When we came to the church, I took a start.

"What is the matter?" she asked, breaking the silence.

"That is the shape of the trees and stones I saw in the Agora." It was a small Byzantine church, square, with a terra-cotta roofed dome on pendentives; in the arches of the pendentives hung three large bells. "Have you been to the Agora?" I asked.

She looked at me quizzically. "I didn't think Americans believed in miracles."

"Do *you*?"

"I believe what I see," and Georgia headed into the church, as if she was afraid to remain outside, or simply impatient. I followed her in, past a woman dressed in black seated behind a high counter; she stared ahead, as if blind. Past the wooden offering box. The interior, from floor to ceiling, was covered with paintings, frescos, mosaics, and icons. The figures seemed to move in the flickering candle light; I felt claustrophobic, even though the main room was large and high-ceilinged, for I could feel the weight of the years in this place. A thousand years of art and devotion. The prayers of the dead filled the space like millions of invisible feathers. They were the shadows, the jittery guttering of votive candles, dim reflections on silver and gold. Every wall and ceiling was covered with painted figures: on the upper walls was the celestial hierarchy dominated by a gold haloed Christ—a shadow Pantocrantor waiting for the first strong rays of

morning light to proclaim his majesty; the Virgin Mary stood in the eastern apse, half hidden in darkness, as if she were naked and shy; and as I gazed upon her, I knew where the old Greek gods were hiding, for she was Hera, and, perhaps, Aphrodite thinly disguised. I moved from room to room, and the ancient figures in the paintings and gold and silver encased icons seemed to shift, to watch me as I passed. I looked at a painting of a saint riding a chariot pulled by sea horses. The water was a flat, faded blue, yet as I looked it deepened, and Saint Poseidon receded, the gold scaling of his halo lightened by grey light streaming in like water from cisterns that were small, high windows. And I could smell the sea; for just that instant it swelled and rippled, as if the painted image had been elevated to hallucination. Details emerged, like figures from a fog, revealing a long shoal descending into the sea. Men and women and children were stepping naked into the water to meet finned angels and cherubim. A Hieronymus Bosch caricature of Heaven.

I heard hurried footsteps behind me.

I called to Georgia, looked for her in the main chapel, and caught up with her outside. The courtyard was filling with people. Despite the size of the crowd, no one spoke.

"Why did you leave without telling me?" I asked.

"I'm going home," she said, as if that answered my question.

I reached for her arm, and she clasped my hand, pressing it hard. Then she pulled away, as if in revul-

sion.

"Come back to the hotel with me."

"Why?"

Because I didn't want to walk through the streets alone. Because I was anxious, uneasy, frightened by shadows...and miracles. Because I couldn't face going back to my room alone. Because she looked like Sandra. Because she wasn't. Or perhaps it was just humiliation. I couldn't just fuck a whore; I had to have a relationship with her, turn a trick into more than money.

I could not answer.

We walked along the edge of the Plaka, skirting the commercial section: the upscale fashion and textile stores, carpet and glitzy jewellery shops. The city had suddenly come frantically alive with people. It was as if they appeared with the light, explosions of them; and in the humid, polluted morning—the sun a wavery smear in the east—the world roared and stank. Everything was noise and touch and motion: car horns blared, children howled and laughed and chased each other while adults spoke at the top of their lungs and drove their cars and motorcycles and motorbikes as if Jesus himself was directing traffic. It was as if everyone needed to get close to everyone else, to breathe each other's flatulent air, to drive in each other's space, to push, shove, and step over and beside each other; and then we were in the market. Smells of cheese and fish and the musty tang of meat.

Athens had awakened from its night stupor.

Vendors shouted to one another in the flea market.

Businessmen crowded into the central metro stop. A heavy woman with enormous arms and unkempt hair thumped the hood of a car. A motorcyclist drove along the crowded sidewalk straight at us. The roar of machines and people was transformed into a droning, continuous streamer of sound, an exhalation that promised to end but didn't; and I remembered my mother measuring the length of the cicada's buzzing to predict how hot the day would be.

She led me down a narrow street filled with huckster tables selling kitsch: blue stone evil eyes glued onto the handles of miniature brooms, decaled icons of saints, plastic worry beads. She held my hand tightly, so we would not become separated.

"Where are we going?" I asked.

"Home...."

Suddenly the commotion of the street was swallowed, as if we had walked a great distance from the market...from the city. I looked down the narrow street into the green and brown darkness of liana, into the leaves and roots and vines and acid-smelling humus of forest. Rainforest. I felt dizzy, for it was like looking down from a height into its thick green canopy. Below this layer of branch and leaf would be tomb-like silence punctuated by shafts of light; and the boles of trees distorted and disguised by parasitic tubers would create imaginary rooms and corridors, naves and chapels and alters of humus. I watched people walking down the street ahead of us, tentatively stepping over broken blocks of concrete pushed upward by brush

and root and tuber to enter the green shade of forest. I felt warm, as if the trees and shoots and vines ahead were radiating heat...and something else: I felt myself yearning for the green shade.

I walked toward the forest, imagining that Georgia was with me; I felt numbed, intoxicated, and I could hear voices whispering. And, impossibly, as I gazed into this welcoming cave of green, I thought of the sea. I moved closer to hear better, for the rushing shushing-ticking-breathing whispers would not quite resolve into words, yet I was certain that's what they were. Green words, cool as the sea, cool as memory; and I heard my wife Sandra speaking to me, as if she were the mother and I was the child; and I remembered the luminous, night-lit green lawns of a resort in the Catskills. I was six or seven and the grass and trees seemed to glow with their own light...and extend forever in all directions. I could not remember seeing the klieg lights that surely illuminated the grounds.

Just so did the forest at the end of the street seem to glow, as if lit by memory. There, before me, was safe haven. And I could hear the forest and everything in it. Yet even as the tubers broke through cement before me, cracking like branches in a New England ice storm, even as the forest approached me like a green god aswirl in leaves, trunk-tall as the eucalyptus, so tall that the canopy of pale trees blocked out the sun, even then and there, in the blood warm shadows did I look into the heart of the sea.

For there I saw the creatures dreaming....

Home....

Fish creature, do you wait in the sea dreaming forests? Or do you wait in the forests dreaming the sea? Do you have moments or eons to dream the world, this one or your own, while you float in the seas, large as Dorian islands—Skorpios or Madouri or even tree carpeted Meganissi? Is this theater or architecture? Are you here or there?

Yes, you dream.

We can hear you and see you and feel you.

But are these your dreams or our own...?

And where, where are you from...?

What sun's planet?

What watery world?

* * * * * * *

They could not get anywhere near the beach. St. Kilda Road, a grand eight-laned thoroughfare lined with palms, had almost no traffic; yet once they turned west into St. Kilda proper, they found the roads impassable: cars blocked every street, every alleyway. It was as if the Mercedes, Holden Jackaroo Vans, Falcons, Russian Neva Four by Fours, and Lasers had been simply abandoned, some with their engines still running.

"I think we should get out of here," Peter said.

"We're almost there," Mary-Ellen insisted. "We can go up and around and take Jackson Street to the beach."

She backed the car into a driveway and turned around; but she was boxed in, for a 1967 cherry red, mint-condition Chevy Impala convertible was blocking the road.

"I'll see what I can do to get it moved," Peter said. "Whoever owns the damn thing must've just parked it there this minute." Mary-Ellen nodded her head impatiently, as if she had something more important to think about.

Peter got out of the car and for a beat he stood still, like an animal testing the air for sound or smell. There was not a soul around; the street was quiet, except for the thrumming of Mary-Ellen's car...and the empty Chevy, idling loudly in a throaty purr. Peter felt a shiver of fear snake up his back, for something had shifted, just as it had in the rain forest; but it wasn't the eerie quiet or the lack of people on the streets. It was a pervading—and sickening—sense of...permanence and immanence. The atmosphere itself seemed to be different, and there was a whiff of ozone in the air, as if prefiguring a storm. The light was hard and brilliant, seemingly reflecting off every surface to hurt the eyes; yet it cast shadows sharp as compass lines; and it was humid, as humid as in the rain forest; and Peter felt as if he was falling. He hadn't felt that since he had first come to Australia to be with Nedra. He remembered how everything had seemed slightly off center in those first few months, and how often he had felt the urge to cry. As he did now. As if everything precious had suddenly been lost to the past, or to this bright and

hollow future.

He called out to the owner of the Chevy, but no one answered; there was hardly an echo in the empty street. He waited—the polished hood radiated heat like hot tarmac—then got into the convertible and parked it facing away from Mary-Ellen's car. But in that time, in the few seconds that his back was turned to Mary-Ellen, she had disappeared. Unlike the Chevy's owner, she had turned off the ignition and locked the doors— as if to keep Peter out. Peter shouted her name and ran down the street. He had a clear view ahead, but she was nowhere to be seen. Obviously she had cut across to another street; most likely she knew the area. Peter was certain that she would be heading toward the water. He stopped, out of breath and sweating. He could just go back, take the Chevy and try to drive the fuck out of here, perhaps drive through some invisible scrim back into reality; but just now, in the quiet of the streets, he remembered with the force and clarity of hallucination his days and nights in hospital. He smelled the sharp limy tang of the ocean again, the ocean that had filled his recurrent dreams. And now that human and mechanical noise was stilled, he could hear the ocean, could hear its whispers as it breathed and sighed. Could there be something in the ocean calling him against all reason?

He remembered dreaming of the creatures who were themselves dreaming, dreaming the familiar world into something as alien as themselves.

Once again, here was the dream.

He was standing in it, listening to it; and he felt himself being pulled toward the sea. "Nedra, help me," he whispered, pleading, or praying; and somehow it seemed as if he had suddenly awakened, pushing his way out of the dream; and indeed he must have jolted himself awake, for now he could hear a faint roaring in the distance. Was it a crowd by the beach? Or traffic? Or the sea itself?

He hurried through the silent, empty streets toward the sound. He passed the entrance to Luna Park, a bright yellow cement face with a gaping red-lipped mouth; he passed the Palace Theatre and the children's castle with its blue and red and green towers; he walked through terraced neighbourhoods of chockablock terra-cotta roofed houses; until he came to a palm-lined esplanade where he could look down to the beach.

It was as crowded as a hot Saturday. People were milling about the narrow shelf of sand like fleas, and Peter imagined that he was watching a pitched battle, for it seemed as if those closest to the water were being pushed into it, their space on the wet sand immediately possessed by the next rank of citizen soldiers. And the crowd was screaming...no that's wrong, Peter thought. They're calling out to the sea.

To the creatures in the sea....

And Peter looked beyond the thronging crowds, out to the water, beyond, to the other side of the harbour, across to Port Philip Bay where shipbuilding cranes were silhouetted against a flat, blue, cloudless sky. He looked into the water, scanning it like words on paper.

Its inky shoals of dead vegetable matter were purple, bleeding into bands of turquoise and a region of pale blue that could have been mistaken for the sky itself. There he saw the creature, at first mistaking it for an island. He imagined he could hear it, as if it were the sea itself, imagined that what he had thought was the roaringcallingshouting of the crowd was but an echo of the island creature, a public clarion, a megaphone screaming what everyone wanted and yearned to hear.

Destiny revealed.

And Peter, standing away from the massed tumult, away from the eye of the action, away from the crowding thoughts of those below, saw the death and transformation of thousands of ordinary people as peripheral, for he, too, saw and heard the creature.

Saw it through its eyes. Curved expanses of flesh smooth as glass and harder than diamonds; indeed, the creature was transparent, but that was a psychological, not a physiological state. Or perhaps both were the same. Peter saw it as a vague, distant, elliptical shape, but that was overlaid with the image he saw in his mind's eye—the image directed toward him like coherent light by the creature: its greyish pink gill slits shivered, and its vertical tail moved slowly from side to side, and Peter recognised the creature as the enemy. Sharklike, larger than even a whale shark, the largest creature on earth, it stalked him with infinite patience. It drew him down to the beach, bathing him in the radiance of its musing; and Peter could feel an ancient phylogenic urge to return to the sea, back to the watery

womb from which he had been torn.

And so did he walk to the beach, to the crowds, to the sea. He yearned, like the crowds milling around him, to swim and breathe as the creature. The slow, comforting, clock-ticking thoughts of the creature turned the sea and all it's dark depths into a bath. The cold water that would cleanse and transform.

The creature's sea thoughts....

The sea....

Rolling, thrusting white fingers into dark, damp sand, repeating, demanding, controlling....

Still Peter found it in himself to resist.

There *must* be an explanation. Maybe he was caught up in some sort of mass hysteria, or some millennial manifestation of mob behaviour, or perhaps he tried to withstand the creatures' call because he was tied to the dead past and deaf to the present. Or perhaps he was crazy, yes, that was just as plausible; and *Peter remembers a childhood dream.... The dream is in colour; he remembers that. The overwhelming colour is deep blue, and it's night, a flat moonless night; and he is asleep in a bed beside the window of a large mountain cabin. He is on vacation, and Mom and Dad are in the next room. It's the middle of the night. In his dream he wakes up and looks out the window. He has never experienced such silence. It's as if he has suddenly gone deaf; he doesn't hear the familiar night noises: the creaking and groaning of clapboard and shingle, the distant whistle of a train, the cheechee scry of bats; but before he can try to speak and break*

out of the dream, he sees lights falling like petals ever so slowly out of the sky. They are beautiful, perfect, unearthly, and there are so very many of them dropping everywhere. Wherever they fall he can see explosions of soft yellow light. A fluorescence. He cannot imagine anything more beautiful, yet he's suddenly terrified because he knows that something terrible is happening, something terrible and beautiful, something that will change everything forever. But he can't scream himself awake. Instead he watches the lights falling out of the sky by the hundreds....

"*No!*" he screamed, as the crowd pushed, carrying him with them to the sea that was thick with spawning krill and boiling with eels and rays and yabbies and coral reef fish that had never been seen in these waters. Peter's shout seemed deafening, even among the rustling of thousands of people, for it was as if speech had been swallowed by the sea, as if everyone was already under water, already swimming, darting forward, swirling around each other to form a roiling mass. Food for the sea. For the fishes in the sea.

He saw the faces of those around him emptied out by the beast that was an island in the sea. He smelled the bloated corpses, which were strewn all over the wet sand and stepped over without notice, as if they were stones or plastic litter. He smelled the sea, thick with organic perfumes, and then he was in it. The crowd pushed him, carried him, crawled over him, stepped on him, in their common rush to get to deep water.

He could gain no purchase on the sandbar.

He choked and gagged and inhaled water.

He would breathe or drown, dream or die, for like the others he was being pulled into the submerged eye of the shark, into the pale blue of dreams, into sky and sea and transformation. And so he dreamed, as if the cold, living water were itself the stuff of dreams, a conduit of thought that connected Peter to the great shark, the mind and motor of the sea.

But it wasn't either or, it wasn't dream or die; it was breathe or drown, but not as the creature and the sea demanded. He breathed, he inhaled, but not the sea. He pushed and kicked himself to the surface and gasped for air. He fought to stay on the surface, and he swam and treaded water and walked out of the sea onto the corpse-strewn beach. He was alone with the dead, but the shark's dream still clung to him like his sodden clothes. He resisted, yet could not quite walk away from the beach. He felt empty, as he had when Nedra died; and as if the creature and the sea held all his yearnings, he could not completely leave them. Neither would he succumb to their lure. So he made his way to the timber pier, as if the Victorian kiosk at its end was some sort of half way house. Here he would be safe. Here he could watch and try to understand, marooned on this narrow strip that was neither earth nor sea.

Beyond the kiosk was a curving rock breakwater, usually occupied by penguins and sea birds. But not today. Peter leaned over the railing: thousands of people were now swimming underwater without coming up for air. Some still wore their clothes, but most were

naked; and Peter glimpsed the new, raw slashes in their necks—gill slits. Reflexively he felt his own neck, felt the raised spots that ached and burned, but his flesh had not opened, for he had resisted. He watched the swimmers; their legs and feet had already fused together—a grotesque renunciation of earth and air and sky.

Flesh transformed by a thought, flesh evolving toward the watery womb, a miracle of flesh finned flesh gilled flesh: a gift from creatures as distant as Heaven.

Peter gazed, transfixed, into the water at the finned and gilled men and women and children; he could see the vague shapes of corpses in the shallows below, those who could not or would not be transformed. Their arms waved, as they danced with eels and crabs in the undertow. Below, by the pylons of the pier, a woman rose to the surface, gasping for air, flailing her arms above the water. She looked like Mary-Ellen, but he could not be sure; and then she slid downward into the grey-green water, into the purpling depths.

He could still feel the creature's cold thoughts beating against him like curlers on a beach....

"It's been happening like this all day."

Startled, Peter turned to find a balding man in a black suit. He spoke with an American accent, and his shoulders were hunched, as if he found being tall an embarrassment. He wore black thick-framed plastic glasses and had uneven teeth that were so white they might have been caps. His full moustache exaggerated his thin face, which was an expanse of forehead, gaunt cheeks, and a cleft chin.

"You've been here all day?" Peter asked.

"Most of it. They come down to the beach and walk into the sea." The man turned his head slightly, indicating that he meant those who were now swimming. "But they don't stay long." He stepped beside Peter and leaned against the rail. "See?"

Peter looked down. Indeed, the swimmers were gone, as were the corpses. As if they had never been.

"They come in waves. You came in with the last of them. You were the straggler, that's why you didn't find anyone on the streets."

"How did you get here?" Peter asked, suddenly frightened, sensing something deadly and dangerous and close.

The man chuckled. "Same way you did. It's jubilee. Soon *you'll* be down there. How long can you resist the inevitable?"

"Who are you?" Peter asked, looking up quickly; but there was no one there.

Had been no one there....

Only the creature swimming toward him, sending its waves to beat upon the beach like tendrils of thought, sending itself like Christ to the man who would not listen.

* * * * * * *

I woke up exhausted in the darkness of my hotel room. I had been having fever dreams; and for an instant, as I hung between the borders of sleep and wakefulness, I was in the rain forest. I could smell its

rich vapours—the flowering lianas, the gagging fish-rot of a river that twisted and disappeared, tree mush-rooms blooming and decaying, dampness cloying, enveloping, misting my skin until I could not bear my sweat-soaked clothes. I wanted to leave them behind, throw them away...as Georgia did.

I bolted fully awake.

Georgia....

I sat up on the bed, shivering in a cold sweat, and pulled off my soaking undershirt. I turned on the light on the night table, but the room seemed to grow huge, and I quickly switched off the lamp. Blazing white afterimages receded to grey, and as my heart slowed, I remembered....

I remembered walking into the green mirage at the end of the narrow street in the Plaka flea market. Georgia walked with me—walked across the broken street that was being crushed, overwhelmed, by root and leaf and fern—walked with me into the rain forest. The dim rooms and rows and phantasms created by the great-boled trees were but manifestations of yearning itself, and so we were drawn, pulled, sucked into the silent, sweating shade, into the soft, life-giving sunlight of immanence radiated by fronds and boles and tubers, by the jewelled insects and scurrying beasts, by vipers slipping through grotto blue river water, by salamanders glittering along the banks. Monkeys hung shining on branches, prey for eagles that were, in turn, like reflected sunlight on the water below them. Clouds of parrots, glowing, flew overhead, tiny stars

in a living, moving constellation; and Georgia beside me, sweating and pulling me along, overtaking the others, who moved slowly, as if in a trance. She led me through alleys and streets and avenues created by trees and vines that seemed to reach upward forever, along the leaf-mulched floor of the forest, toward a narrow gap ahead...a blue eye unblinking...a hole, a tear in the silent living creature that was the rain forest. It grew as we pressed toward it. There were no human tracks here, just those of jaguar, ocelot, and panther; and not a sound could be heard, except for the crunching of twigs and leaves beneath our feet. Even the cicadas were silenced. And I remember that my heart was beating quickly, not from fear but anticipation.

And the eye grew larger, revealing itself as sky, as sea the colour of sky, as if one were merely the reflection of the other. There, as rain forest ended—a living, breathing, green wall—we padded along soft sandy beach toward the sea, toward the creatures as large as islands that were waiting, willing, dreaming. Dreaming the forest and the sea, dreaming us.

Georgia let go of my hand and ran ahead toward the sea, toward the creatures. I watched her strip off her dress and fall into the sea, as if into a mirror. I could feel her joy, hear the creatures that were coaxing me to follow. They whispered like thought itself, as if they were the memories of ancient conversations. Georgia did not turn back; overcome with bliss, she left me without a glance, and I...I ran back through the forest, which now seemed suddenly dark and dead

and dangerous. I ran back to the street, to the crowds milling in the market, back to the hotel, here....

I closed my eyes, trying to clear my head of memories, then got up and walked across the room to the balcony. I threw open the doors, expecting a rush of air and noise. It was quiet, silent, and the air was heavy with musk and perfume, the damp, sweet smells of rain forests, of jungle. The familiar acrid smell of Athens' pollution had disappeared. The city had stopped. Yet below me, in the street, I saw water purling once again over cobblestones and steps, lapping against cement rails, perrons, and brick walls. But this time my eyes weren't being tricked by light and mist and humidity. Water was indeed streaming through the lamp-lit streets. What I had glimpsed from the balcony earlier, as Georgia had closed her arms around me for 50,000 drachmas, had now coalesced into reality.

Were the creatures in the sea dreaming this into being? Was this my own private dream of coursing water and death? Or was it some watery manifestation of Athens' collective yearning? I could only watch and listen, expecting to hear voices in the breeze, in the water below, for, of course, I was dreaming.

I had to be dreaming.

Only in a dream could reality twist and change like this. Only in a dream could I look on, unafraid; and, as if I had given myself the suggestion, I felt a vertiginous longing and emptiness. Georgia, why hadn't I followed you? Why did I turn and run? I clung to a tiny core in myself that rejected the security, the empty

warmth, the longing for transformation. I wanted the world back, the world we had made, the failed, imperfect, human world. I thought of Sandra and reached inside myself, searching for familiar pain...the pain I had tried to run away from, the pain that could not be undone with a wink and a nod; but it was lost, buried, hidden. Stolen. Sandra was a name, a familiar smell, a recollection; and I knew as I watched the water purling below, that even if I could wake up and find the fear that had saved me from the beast, it would, eventually, draw me back to the sea, to itself.

I listened. Silent Athens. The city lights looked hazy, haloed, blinking like stars obscured by clouds. I needed to see people, needed to hear conversation, for I could not help but feel that everything had just died, that Athens itself had died, and that I was alone, marooned. No use to pick up the phone as a test and call for Ari. The phone had never worked. And what if I went downstairs? Would the lobby be flooded? How deep the water...? *Wake up*! I struck the desk with my fist, hard, and felt the pain radiate up my arm.

I was awake.

I dressed, went downstairs, and found Ari. He was sitting in the lobby behind his desk, which was perched on a ledge joined to the staircase. He wore an open shirt that looked soiled and wrinkled; he had undoubtedly slept in it. His face was flushed, and his hair was dishevelled, revealing his bald spot, usually carefully covered with long strands of pomaded hair. He held a glass, probably Ouzo, in both hands.

"Greetings, Mister Blackford. *Kali-ni-hta*. Would you like a drink? On the house." He smiled hopefully. "Come, we will go into the bar. I have scotch if you do not wish Ouzo. It is only you and me left in the hotel and—" He gestured toward the door, at the water running along the street.

I nodded and walked down the few steps into the lobby foyer. The door was closed, but as it was mostly glass, I had a clear view of the street. The stream, although shallow, was filled with fish sliding under the oily water like shadows. I could see cod, bass, white-bait, mullet, and eels. There were small silvery fish in profusion, swirling, reflecting schools of them swimming below bobbing, plastic bottles and bits of paper.

"The water here is not deep," Ari said, as if the stream seething with fish was a perfectly natural phenomenon. "It has not yet come over the front steps to the hotel. However, in some streets you need a boat. I have seen it. Like Venice, is it not?"

"Like Venice," I said, glad to be following Ari into the combination bar and breakfast room.

"But we have time," Ari insisted. "This is as good a place to be as any. Did you not see the fish swimming in the street? You would not be hungry here. Would you like me to cook you a fish? I would not charge you. After all, it is from God, is it not?"

I declined his offer, and we sat down at a table. Ari brought glasses, a bottle of scotch, and a bottle of Ouzo. "Where are the other guests?"

He laughed sourly, then took a large swallow of

Ouzo. It was transparent in his glass, which meant he had not bothered to add the traditional splash of water, which would have turned the liquor cloudy. "They all left to swim with the fish."

"What do you mean?" I asked, although I knew...I knew.

"You won't see them here, of course, for the water is so, uh...undeep." He looked to me for the correct word.

"Shallow."

"Ah, yes, 'shallow,'" Ari said. "Only good for small fishes. But go to Syntagmatos Street. You can stand on higher ground and see everyone under the water. They are now fish, no longer men. Fish.... But here it is almost dry. You are safe here, Mister Blackford."

"Why are *you* here, Ari?" I asked.

He sighed. "I am waiting for God to take me. But perhaps he does not want me. I think that is so."

"Why don't you go to your family?"

"You cannot drive anywhere now. The streets that are not underwater are filled with cars, all empty. Or covered with jungle. There is jungle, too, Mister Blackford, here, in Athens. Remember the miracle in the Agora? That you told me you did not see? There was a church there. I, too, couldn't see it, but many did. It's big now. A cathedral." He crossed himself. "I looked, but I couldn't see it."

"What did you see?" I asked.

"Jungle, all the way up the hill to the Acropolis, too. Big trees—and birds and animals and flowers—such as have never been seen in Greece."

"Then you've seen the...miracle."

"No, it is not the same, Mister Blackford. For you, I could understand, you're a Jew. So—I mean no disrespect, Mister Blackford—it could be understood why you would not see the church, or the cathedral. But I am a Christian. But a bad one. So, you see. Here we are." He tried to refill my glass, but I stopped him.

"So there are others like us," I said, but it was a question.

Ari shrugged. "Probably...some. But everyone is in the water or in the jungle. So quickly, no?" He laughed, as if he had just thought of a joke.

Had Ari and I rejected this new world...or had it rejected us, leaving us to become outcasts on deserted islands?

I stood up to leave.

"Maybe it will change, Mister Blackford," he said. "Maybe it will go back to the way it was before...before God. Maybe everyone will come back."

"Maybe they will."

"Maybe we are here to take care of everything in the meantime." Again he laughed, sourly. Then he said, a touch of desperation in his voice, "Stay here. It's good as any place."

"I'll have a look around. Perhaps I'll come back."

As I stood up to leave, he said, "None of the others came back...."

* * * * * * *

Peter Lindsay retraced his steps, walked back past

Luna Park, past the Palace Theatre and the pastel painted children's castle, walked down the neatly kept streets of terra-cotta roofed houses, working his way through the seemingly endless traffic jam of empty cars...cars that had been parked on the streets and sidewalks and lawns. He walked quickly, and his footsteps echoed like shots, for he was alone here, completely and absolutely alone. It was as if the sea and sky had swallowed everything alive, yet Peter could still feel a presence.

As if the man on the pier were right behind him, stalking him. A ghost.

But Peter sensed a change as he approached St. Kilda Road. The air seemed to clear, to become lighter and drier, as if humidity and its accompanying whiff of ozone were the messengers of dreams. He saw someone walking, walking ahead, threading his way through parked cars, pausing here and there, as if to decide which one to take. Here was another human being, someone who could walk and breathe and swing his arms. Peter called out to the figure. The man stopped, turned to look at him, then disappeared down another street; and for one terrible instant, Peter imagined that it was the same man he had seen on the pier: another phantasm, a creation of the sea.

But suddenly he heard traffic, the plashing of tires, a distant white noise that made him homesick for his own home just miles from here, homesick for his own familiar things. He wanted to shave and wash his face with his own towel. He wanted to make a cup of tea,

listen to the traffic on Punt Road, look at his collection of prints and paintings that covered his walls, assure himself that there still was a familiar world of small comforts.

As he approached the last of the cars left in the road, he saw a green Jaguar convertible. The top was down, the keys in the ignition. He checked the glove compartment, found the registration papers. Thank God it wasn't Stephen's. He'd call when he got home. If he could get home.

Without a qualm, he drove the Jaguar down the empty street, turned onto St. Kilda, and after a few long, palm-lined blocks, found himself in traffic...cars stopping at intersections, people dressed in business clothes walking by on sidewalks, business as usual. Nothing had changed here; and he drove west home. Couples jogged along elm shaded lanes, an old man fed popcorn to the pigeons, high school students in red and white uniforms played cricket.

Peter parked the car in front of his house and noticed that in his rush to leave with Stephen he had left the mesh metal gate open. He closed it, stood in his yard for a moment, taking in the familiarity of it all: his rose bushes, small compost pile, the trees that he refused to trim or cut down, although they scratched against his roof and windows in the slightest wind. He looked at Nedra's earthen pots of busy lizzie and flowering cherry. He could almost feel her presence here; and he felt the tears come, along with the curious thunder sound that he always heard inside his head when he

cried. He remembered hearing that sound when he was a child, and now he was sixty-three and still hearing it. *Nedra, I miss you so.* I'll call Stephen, he told himself, opening the door, feeling better at being in surroundings he could control; but as he stepped in the house, he felt a profound exhaustion. He would sleep all of this away, as if it had never happened.

But first he would make himself a cup of tea.

* * * * * * *

You whisper to them, you embrace them. Even as they call your name, you devour them. You draw them down. Into the depths where the stars burn.
Reefs of them.
Dreaming.

* * * * * * *

I made my way down Nikkis Street through water that was well above my ankles and hoped I could get back to the Agora. The eels and schools of shiny small fish gave me wide berth, but I could feel crayfish being crushed underfoot. It was easy to get lost in this maze of narrow, winding streets, which were already turning into canals. Indeed, Athens was turning into Venice, an empty Venice. There was not another soul on the street, and I imagined that this watery city was a machine, a great neon clockwork automatically ticking away. That it was empty was but a minor detail. The lights in the shops were on. The street lamps were bright. Except

for the fish swimming through the dark water that streamed down the street, everything seemed dead. I could not hear the creatures of the sea that had whispered to me in my dreams...or their dreams. I was deaf, isolated, as if I were being punished for not following Georgia into the sea.

The water receded as I made my way back to the Agora, which was dry. The streets had been broken by roots. Slabs of concrete had buckled, there were hills of ancient cobblestones, and, of course, the great trees. I could not tell where the high chain-link fence had stood, which had enclosed the ancient temple stones... which had enclosed the church I had seen, the mirage formed from the impossibilities of root and vine and leaf. Perhaps the fence still stood, buried in the tangled, humid, woody darkness ahead. Yet street lamps blazed in the humid air, as if the creatures of this new world had left them on so they could see their handiwork. A child walked out of an alley toward the rain forest, which was claiming everything west of Athinas Street. I called to him, ran after him, but he disappeared into the shadow tangle of the Agora like a cherub passing into heaven.

I stopped before the upheavals of stone and cement. I could hear them cracking and breaking, and I could hear the groaning of wood and vine as they reached upward, grasping tendrils, connecting and thickening and melding into every other leafy limb and torso. Giving birth in that connection to the silent beasts and reptiles, to the birds and insects wriggling in the soil

and forming clouds in the spore infected air.

And as I stared into the rain forest, into the darkness, for it looked to me like a well, a pit, I began to make out the outlines of Ari's cathedral, and as I stared at it, so did it seem to gain substance, and the forest began to fluoresce, as if covered with the microscopic phosphorescent organisms that set beaches and water aglow on summer nights, fluoresced into the organic flowing lines of a Gothic cathedral...into flying buttresses supporting flowering vaults—living, growing scaffolding—into naves, defined by thin boles and fronds, into spires and pinnacles, towers and gables and galleries and arches, all reaching like a hundred towers integrated into one shifting, knotted structure. Here were Reims and Sainte-Chapelle and St. Maclou combined.

If I entered, I might be lost. But what else was there to do? Wait for God with Ari and drown? Wait for the creatures to speak? Wait for dreams while getting drunk on Ouzo?

But the simple truth was that I *wanted* to go.

I wanted to feel once again the warm, green security. In fact, I yearned for the intoxicating, numbing bliss, for the whisperings and soft corridors of dream, for secret conversations profoundly sensed and heard in the susurration and ululation of leaf and sea; and I yearned to see Georgia, whom I imagined as a long, lithe mermaid, a naiad transformed, rather than one of Ari's grotesque "fish."

I entered the vined cathedral, walked through naves

and chapels and transepts of glowing vines, palms, and dead spinifex. I walked along a dark trail, confined by a great vine forest on either side of me that was like two receding walls; although it was the dark of night, a suffusing glow of trees and fronds extended away from me in all directions. But I was being led along a dead path, a pavement of bones and shells and spongy dirt that was the residue of rot. I heard no voices, no whispers of comfort, and I felt the isolation and despair of the damned. I had turned away from the warmth and succouring light, and now it was being withheld, even now while I walked in the belly of the beast, as I followed the way I had taken with Georgia. Around me, everything had crystallised into silence, and I imagined that if I tapped any of the twisted tree limbs or huge veined fronds that glittered as I passed, I would send a reverberation through this tangled, twisted beast, would set this glacier of forms a-shiver. And it would shatter around me, the branches becoming spears of beryl and jade and emerald. But there was no life here as there had been before, no animals padding, no birds or insects made out of light. No sound but my feet crunching upon dead matter.

I came to a river, which was as glassy as winter ice. Mushrooms scattered along its banks looked like frosted jewels or colored baubles. I had seen this river before, with Georgia. We had passed it. Now it glowed like the quiet water in Capri's Blue Grotto, and there led my path. To the creatures in the sea? To Georgia?

I looked for a blue parting in the forest, looked

for the sea that would glow even in the night, for the sea that had accepted Georgia; and then, suddenly, I understood. I was still inside the cathedral, which now began to pulse with life, as if needing only recognition. The river was glass, part of the *ars de geometria* that curved overhead; and the translucent trees were but large mullions that separated enormous stained glass windows. As I looked through the forest turned to glass—to ice that radiated heat and light—I could see the blue of sky and sea through the branches and fronds and vines.

And I walked out of the forest into sunlight, into eternal day. Before me was a long shoal descending into a faded blue sea, and ahead were familiar figures, the same ones that I had gazed upon when Georgia had taken me to her church. Here were the images and icons I had seen on the walls come to life: the finned angels standing in the shallows, watching, and the naked supplicants—the men and women and children— waiting on the beach. Here was Georgia—her hair long and wet, her skin pale as porcelain—welcoming me, giving me another chance.

I knew this place. I had been here before.

This was the island of Lefkada, near the fabled palace of the old wanderer Odysseus. I could see the smaller islands of Madouri, Skorpios, and dark Meganisi in the hazy blue distance. But there were also other islands floating like mirages in the clear calm water, islands I had never seen before, islands as smooth as stone...or glass.

I called out to Georgia.

I called to her as I walked into the sea that was viscous, heavy as oil.

I called to her as the islands—glass smooth creatures—moved toward me, swallowing oceans and pumping them back through gill slits high as cathedrals.

I called to her....

* * * * * * *

Peter turned on the electric kettle, dropped a tea bag in his mug, and then looked out the kitchen window, expecting to see the neighbour's white cement house, red and gold flowers, cars parked on both sides of the street.

But there was no house, no street.

There was water. Ocean. Perpendicular cliffs and gorges and great waves crashing, attacking, grinding and wearing down rock walls to create huge castles and spires and towers: detached cliffs rising from the sea, from the reefs.

From his kitchen window, Peter looked out at the cliffs and rock stacks and ocean. Looked out at the creature in the sea, a creature larger than any of the rock stacks. A creature transparent as glass. A heat distortion in the water. An aberration of light curving into the smooth shape of a whale shark. Waiting.

The rocks looked purple in the sunset. The red sky filled with twisted braids of yellow clouds; and the ocean was undulating, expanding and contracting, as if

it were breathing, as if it contained all the dark depths of space...a void without stars, the ultimate darkness.

Peter turned away from the window. The light on the electric kettle blinked on, indicating that the water was hot. He walked out of the kitchen, through the living room, where Stephen had left the suitcases, and into the studio, which smelled of oil and varnish and turpentine and the reassuring sweet musk of memory. He pulled the drawstring of the pleated linen window blinds and prayed for a view of the neighbour's yellow townhouse.

But he found only the sea.

ABOUT THE AUTHOR

JACK DANN is a multiple award-winning author who has written or edited over seventy-five books, including the groundbreaking novels *Junction, Starhiker, The Man Who Melted, The Memory Cathedral*—which was an international bestseller—the Civil War novel *The Silent*, and *Bad Medicine*, which has been compared to the works of Jack Kerouac and Hunter S. Thompson, and called "the best road novel since the *Easy Rider* days."

Dann's work has been compared to Jorge Luis Borges, Roald Dahl, Lewis Carroll, Castaneda, Ray Bradbury, J. G. Ballard, Mark Twain, and Philip K. Dick. Dick, the author of the stories from which the films *Blade Runner* and *Total Recall* were made, wrote that "*Junction* is where Ursula K. Le Guin's *The Lathe of Heaven* and Tony Boucher's 'The Quest for Saint Aquin' meet...and yet it's an entirely new novel.... I may very well be basing some of my future work on *Junction*." Best selling author Marion Zimmer Bradley called *Starhiker* "a superb book...it will not give up all its delights, all its perfections, on one reading."

Library Journal has called Dann "...a true poet who

can create pictures with a few perfect words." Roger Zelazny thought he was a reality magician, and *Best Sellers* has said that "Jack Dann is a mind-warlock whose magicks will confound, disorient, shock, and delight." *The Washington Post Book World* compared his novel *The Man Who Melted* with Ingmar Bergman's film *The Seventh Seal*.

His books have been widely translated, and his short stories have appeared in *Playboy, Omni, Penthouse, Asimov's,* "*Best of*" collections in Australia, the United States, and Great Britain, and other major magazines and anthologies. He is the editor of the anthology *Wandering Stars*, one of the most acclaimed American anthologies of the 1970s, and several other well-known anthologies such as *More Wandering Stars. Wandering Stars* and *More Wandering Stars* have recently been reprinted in the U.S. Dann also edited the multi-volume *Magic Tales* series with Gardner Dozois and is a consulting editor for Tor Books.

He is a recipient of the Nebula Award, the Australian Aurealis Award (twice), the Ditmar Award (four times), the World Fantasy Award, the Peter McNamara Achievement Award, the Peter McNamara Convenors Award for Excellence, and the *Premios Gilgamés de Narrativa Fantástica* award. Dann has also been honored by the Mark Twain Society (Esteemed Knight).

High Steel, a novel co-authored with Jack C. Haldeman II, was published in 1993 by Tor Books. Critic John Clute called it "a predator...a cat with blazing eyes gorging on the good meat of genre. It is

most highly recommended." Dann is currently writing *Ghost Dance*, the sequel to *High Steel*, with Jack Haldeman's widow, author Barbara Delaplace.

Dann's major historical novel about Leonardo da Vinci—entitled *The Memory Cathedral*—was published to rave reviews. It has been published in over ten languages to date. It won the Australian Aurealis Award, was #1 on *The Age* bestseller list, and a story based on the novel was awarded the Nebula Award. *The Memory Cathedral* was also shortlisted for the Audio Book of the Year, which was part of the Braille & Talking Book Library Awards.

Morgan Llewelyn called *The Memory Cathedral* "a book to cherish, a validation of the novelist's art and fully worthy of its extraordinary subject." *The San Francisco Chronicle* called it "A grand accomplishment," *Kirkus Reviews* thought it was "An impressive accomplishment," and *True Review* said, "Read this important novel, be challenged by it; you literally haven't seen anything like it."

Dann's novel about the American Civil War, *The Silent*, was chosen as one of *Library Journal's* 'Hot Picks'. *Library Journal* wrote: "This is narrative storytelling at its best—so highly charged emotionally as to constitute a kind of poetry from hell. Most emphatically recommended." Peter Straub said "This tale of America's greatest trauma is full of mystery, wonder, and the kind of narrative inventiveness that makes other novelists want to hide under the bed." And *The Australian* called it "an extraordinary achievement."

His novel *Bad Medicine* (titled *Counting Coup* in the U.S.), a contemporary road novel, has been described by *The Courier Mail* as "perhaps the best road novel since the Easy Rider Days."

Dann is also the co-editor (with Janeen Webb) of the groundbreaking Australian anthology, *Dreaming Down-Under*, which Peter Goldsworthy called "the biggest, boldest, and most controversial collection of original fiction ever published in Australia." It won Australia's Ditmar Award and was the first Australian book ever to win the World Fantasy Award. His anthology, *Gathering the Bones*, of which he is a co-editor, was included in *Library Journal*'s Best Genre Fiction of 2003, and was shortlisted for The World Fantasy Award. His anthology, *Wizards*, co-edited with Gardner Dozois, and titled *Dark Alchemy* in the UK and Australia, made the Waldenbooks/Borders bestseller list, and was shortlisted for the World Fantasy Award. He has also edited a sequel to *Dreaming Down-Under*: *Dreaming Again*. The influential *Bookseller+Publisher* gave *Dreaming Again* a five star rating and wrote: "Here are stories that engage with the building blocks of our culture and others that give shape to our shared darkness and light. *Dreaming Again* is at once quintessentially Australian and enticingly other. If you read short fiction you'll want this collection. If you don't, this is a reason to start."

His most recent anthologies are *Dreaming Again*, *The Dragon Book* (with Gardner Dozois), *Australian Legends* (with Jonathan Strahan), and *Ghosts by*

Gaslight (with Nick Gevers).

Dann's stories have been collected in *Timetipping*, *Visitations*, and the retrospective short story collection *Jubilee: the Essential Jack Dann*. *The West Australian* said it was "Sometimes frightening, sometimes funny, erudite, inventive, beautifully written and always intriguing. *Jubilee* is a celebration of the talent of a remarkable storyteller." His collaborative stories can be found in his collection *The Fiction Factory*.

The *West Australian* called Dann's recent novel, *The Rebel: An Imagined Life of James Dean*, "an amazingly evocative and utterly convincing picture of the era, down to details of the smells and sensations—and even more importantly, the way of thinking." *Locus* wrote: "*The Rebel* is a significant and very gripping novel, a welcome addition to Jack Dann's growing oeuvre of speculative historical novels, sustaining further his long-standing contemplation of the modalities of myth and memory. This is alternate history with passion and difference." A companion James Dean short story collection entitled *Promised Land* has also been published in Great Britain, as has Dann's most recent short novel, *The Economy of Light*.

As part of its *Bibliographies of Modern Authors Series*, The Borgo Press has published an annotated bibliography and guide entitled *The Work of Jack Dann*. An updated second edition is in progress. Dann is also listed in *Contemporary Authors* and the *Contemporary Authors Autobiography Series*; *The International Authors and Writers Who's Who*;

Personalities of America; *Men of Achievement*; *Who's Who in Writers, Editors, and Poets, United States and Canada*; *Dictionary of International Biography*; the *Directory of Distinguished Americans*; *Outstanding Writers of the 20th Century*; and *Who's Who in the World*. His recently published autobiography is entitled *Insinuations*.

Dann lives in Australia on a farm overlooking the sea, and 'commutes' back and forth to Los Angeles and New York. He is married to the writer Janeen Webb.

His website is jackdann.com. You can also follow him on Twitter @jackmdann